For Jordan,
With very best wishes
I hope you enj

A Missing Mother

A Story of Childhood Loss

Joy Coutts

To my Mother Valerie,
And my brother Paddy.

I dedicate Marianne's story to those who, like us,
experienced the childhood loss of their mother.

And to all mothers that went away too soon... we always miss you.

ISBN 978-1-09838-353-4 eBook 978-1-09838-354-1

CONTENTS

Valérie

Christmas 1942

Their last Christmas together was a fun filled, if frugal occasion. Valérie called it their make do and mend Christmas. They were a family on that special day – her mum Winnie, her dad Phillipe, and her little daughter Marianne. Her Aunt Ethel with her cousin Martin, who was home on leave, arrived with his wife Jean and their son David. The sound of excited children chattering and playing rang around the house. It brought a smile to the adults' faces as the war was forgotten about for a few hours. It pleased Valérie that Marianne had someone to play with: it was good for her in these frightening times.

Valérie asked Martin and Jean to bring some coal and some extra seats with them. That Christmas morning her father lit a blazing fire in the grate and kept it going in the front sitting room all day with the extra fuel in the bucket. The room was usually a rather cold and damp place through under use. The coal sparked and cracked as it heated the room through. Next Phillipe had busied himself constructing a makeshift trestle table in the centre of the room. He kept popping in and out to make sure that the fire kept burning. It was a proper occasion to use the front room in those days. It was only kept for special events or if they had visitors. The fire radiated warmth and joy into all the rooms as good cheer crept through the house and into their hearts.

There were fewer presents to open that year, but Marianne's new toy from grandpa Phillipe and grandma Winnie was a real hit. She was ecstatic as she unwrapped the rag doll with blue button eyes and a calico dress. They had wrapped it up in some crinkled reused paper and string. Winnie had kept it since the beginning of the war. The child was not aware that the scarcities of war extended even to a Ministry of Supply decree that 'no retailer shall provide any paper for the packing or wrapping of goods except for foodstuffs or articles which the shopkeeper has agreed to deliver.' Nor did the little blue-eyed girl care. The new doll found herself hugged and played with all day long.

"So what are you going to call her?" Phillipe asked Marianne as she discarded the paper, not knowing that it would survive to be used again, another day.

"She's called Sammy."

"But that's a boy's name," said David.

"I want her to be Sammy." Valérie recognised her daughter's growing stubborn streak about making her own decisions.

"You call her whatever you like Marianne," said Valérie, "She's your doll and your friend."

"Do you want to come and play with me and Sammy, David?"

"Yeh, alright... my cowboys and Indians can try to shoot your doll and you can run away," said her cousin. The children scampered into the hallway and set up camp at the foot of the stairs.

"When the war is over, we will have the lovely things we used to have before - some oranges and nuts and a bigger Christmas tree. But in the meantime, we'll make do and enjoy the fact that we're all together when so many are away from home this Christmas. It was a good idea when your father planted the tree from a few years ago and then to dig it up every year. Heaven knows we couldn't have afforded one now, even if we could have got hold of one," said Winnie.

"Thank you for inviting us all, I know our contributions are small, but if we share everything out, then we should be able to make a decent meal, Winnie."

"Ethel, there'll be enough to create a feast, I'm sure... you must be on friendly terms with your butcher though, to have got us a chicken. Thank you, it'll do the children good to have a hearty meal. Right now Val, you can come and help me prepare the dinner. Jean, would you set the table, please? You'll find the best china and cutlery in the sideboard there and the tablecloth is in the drawer... you could help too our Martin and give Ethel a day off." Winnie winked at Ethel.

"Of course we can."

"And she'll find me another job to do if I sit still too long," said Phillipe.

"You can keep the fire going, Mr Bouchard, if it's not too much like hard work."

Valérie smiled at the easy chatter between her parents. They never shouted or argued with each other, well not that she ever saw. Their marriage was a solid working partnership and as she watched them together, she knew she had truly tested them over recent years. They had supported her when she had dropped the bombshell of her unmarried pregnancy. And she knew she could never repay them for their help and provision of a roof over hers and Marianne's heads. Their love for each other stretched out and held her and Marianne in its circle too.

"And after dinner lets sing some carols and play some games before the King makes his Christmas speech on the wireless set."

As each family member busied themselves with their chores, Valérie knew that her family would make the best of what they had today. And that the memory of it would carry them through this seemingly never ending war for a few more weeks. The one thing that they had was an abundance of family love. Not even Hitler, his army and his bombs could take that away from them today. She hoped that there wouldn't be any wailing air raid sirens and hiding in the shelter in the garden to interrupt their day together.

The smell of cooking permeated the house, and morning soon turned into afternoon. The children ran around and argued and shouted in their excitement.

"Rightio, I will serve dinner up in five minutes Val, will you sort the children out?"

Her mother was always in control in her kitchen. It was her world, her kingdom. Valérie doubted she would ever learn the knack of having all the ingredients of a hot dinner ready at the same time.

"Come on Marianne, David – wash your hands before your dinner, it's nearly ready," ordered Valérie.

"But Mummy, my hands aren't dirty, I haven't been playing outside... just with Sammy and David."

"Wash them before your dinner silly because they have germs on them, and they might go in your mouth and poison you, and then you'll die." David took a delighted devilment in scaring his slightly younger cousin.

"You probably won't die from germs David, don't exaggerate, but you'd be poorly," said Valérie to her nephew, "Don't frighten her like that, David."

The children's hands eventually washed, everyone took their seats at the table. A flushed and proud Winnie served their Christmas dinner with the help of Valérie.

Phillipe cleared his throat. "We will have a toast," he said as he raised his glass, "Happy Christmas."

A resounding "Happy Christmas" rang around the warm room.

"And to our family," said Valérie.

The grown-ups all lifted their glasses again.

"Now then, let's forget the war today and enjoy our dinner," Winnie urged them.

"Mummy, this is the best dinner I've ever had, shall I save some for tomorrow?"

Marianne's question stopped Valérie in her tracks, her fork suspended in mid-air. She saw the reality of her four-year-old daughter's world. That she was learning so young about not having enough food stabbed at her heart. She placed her fork on her plate and put her arm around her daughter.

"No, you eat it all today if you want to, we will have enough for tomorrow."

Valérie looked across the table to her mother and then her father. Silently they nodded their heads to her. They had sealed a pact.

"So Valérie," said Martin at the same time as devouring some mashed potato, "Aunty Win tells me you've joined the WAAF... the Co-op will miss you, I'm sure."

"Mmm, did she now? I didn't think that I'd actually decided, but it appears I have."

Valérie laughed and glanced at her mother and father.

"Of course you have cherie - the Government needs people like you Val. We need to clear France of the invaders. They are uninvited and not welcome in my homeland. I would return home and I'd fight them myself if I could, but I'm too old now and my family needs me here."

"Phillipe, I said no talk of the war and politics today please."

Winnie scolded him. Phillipe winked at his daughter. He'd always been on her side and devoted himself to her causes too. Valérie sometimes felt sorry for her mother, as she and her father always got their own way with Winnie by joining forces.

"Yes, they can make use of my French skills to listen to the messages coming from the Continent... I can be more useful doing that than listening to women moaning about the price of things and the shortages in the shop."

"Have they replaced you at the Co-op Val? I'd really like to go out and do some work, do my bit."

Valérie noticed the tentativeness in Jean's voice.

Martin looked at his wife in surprise, "I don't know about that Jean, I mean, who'll look after David if you're out all day working? And who'll look after me when I come home?"

"But I'm not doing my bit Martin, stuck at home in the house... women are out working now, the world has changed with nearly all the men away in the war... If I can get someone to help look after David for a while then I'll be able to get a job."

The echo of frustration was loud and clear in Jean's voice. And she understood Jean's need to contribute something, however small, to the war effort.

"Look, both of you," piped up Aunt Ethel, "I'm sure that between us, Winnie and me... well, we can look after our David and Marianne while you girls go out to work, can't we Win?"

"But Jean - we should look after David, he's our son and -" Martin's protest went unheard.

"Another little one to look after won't make any difference to us, will it Philippe?"

Ignoring her nephew's comment, Winnie glanced at Valérie and Jean in solidarity. Valérie knew her father would support the suggestion.

"Of course we can," said Phillipe, "Now let's talk about this later and enjoy our dinner, superbly cooked by my dear wife."

Valérie smiled at her father, grateful for his easy going yet authoritative way of diffusing the tense situation.

"Yes, thank you Mum, this is delicious. And thank you dad for the vegetables from the garden, these new potatoes are tasty."

A silence descended on the room, interrupted only by the sound of the scraping knives and forks against their plates.

"I'll clear away and wash up Mum, you put your feet up in front of the fire. Marianne, David, you can come and help too," said Valérie.

"Ooh no, can't we just play Aunty Valérie? I don't have to help at home, my Mum does all of that kitchen work." David's protest confirmed her suspicions: her nephew was over indulged and was in danger of turning into a mini version of his father.

"No, you and Marianne can play after we wash up the dishes and put away. Now, gather all the knives and forks and put them in the sink, I'll bring the plates."

"Thanks Val, you'll have to be quick though, the King will be on the wireless in twenty minutes." Her mum gave her a grateful smile.

"We will... Jean, do you want to come and give me a hand as well?"

"Yes, I was just about to offer - we don't want to miss the King."

Over the soapy water Valérie washed, and Jean dried. They directed the children to handle the best crockery with care, one piece at a time, and replace it in the sideboard in the sitting room. As they left the kitchen with a plate each, Valérie seized her opportunity.

"Jean, just while the children can't hear: if you really want to go out to work, I'll ask the manager at the Store on Monday if you can take my place."

"Oh, would you Val? Thank you. Martin thinks I should just be a housewife, but I need to do more than just look after the house and David. It's nice having him home on leave for Christmas and all that, but... he's changed since Dunkirk... he's distant and angry... he won't talk to me about it... and it's not fair when he shouts at David, he's still a child... heaven knows what happened to him out there on those beaches."

"Oh Jean, it must have been awful for him and now for you. Of course I'll ask about the job on Monday. You need to get out and meet people... and don't worry between Mum and Dad and Aunt Ethel we will look after David. We'll make it work. When does Martin leave for the front again?"

"Monday morning."

"It's going to be your lucky day, Jean!"

"I can't thank you enough Val."

"You can repay me by looking after Marianne sometime. She can be a right madam sometimes when she thinks she's right, she won't give in. If she believes in something she's like a little terrier with a bone, she won't give it up... heaven help your David if he thinks he's going to tell her what to do."

"I wonder who she takes after?"

Her father came in the back door with a fresh bucket of coal. "Come on girls, have you finished? The King is about to make his broadcast."

They followed him through to the sitting room.

"Shh Marianne, David." Martin was stern with the children.

"Why don't you both play, eh?" said Valérie.

"Can we?" and off Marianne ran into the hallway.

As Valérie took her seat on the woven footstool next to her father, he squeezed her shoulder.

"Shh, I can't hear." Martin chided the adults this time as Jean glanced at her. Valérie winked at her.

Her father turned up the volume dial on the wooden wireless set as the King cleared his throat.

> *"It is at Christmas more than at any other time that we are conscious of the dark shadow of war. Our Christmas festival today must lack many of the happy, familiar features that it has had from our childhood. We miss the actual presence of some of those nearest and dearest, without whom our family gatherings cannot be complete.*
>
> *"But though its outward observances may be limited, the message of Christmas remains eternal and unchanged. It is a message of thankfulness and of hope – of thankfulness to the Almighty for His great mercies, of hope for the return to this earth of peace and goodwill."*

Valérie noticed that while the King talked of the concerted effort of the Allies and cooperation of the countries opposing the invaders, he did not actually mention Germany or Hitler by name.

"So let us welcome the future in a spirit of brotherhood, and thus make a world in which, please God, all may dwell together in justice and peace."

As he ended his speech, Valérie noticed a tear running down her father's cheek. She knew it had broken his heart to hear the news reports from his French homeland just a month ago that the Nazis had also taken the Free Zone of Vichy France under the control of Berlin. It had horrified him to hear Marshall Petain declare that Germany and France had a common goal to defeat England. Phillipe had been quiet for several days after the events. Out of Winnie's earshot he had told Valérie that he could not see France ever being free again after these threatening new events.

But the King's rousing words of brotherhood, the shared sacrifice of the Allied nations and the restoration of peace seemed to have lifted her father's spirits. He jumped up from his armchair.

"I have been saving this for a special occasion," he said as he produced a bottle of brandy from the back of the sideboard. "I think we should have a toast."

Deftly, he filled six small glasses and handed them around.

"As the King said: to peace and justice."

The toast echoed around the room. Everyone felt this Christmas could be the beginning of more peaceful days - certainly more peaceful than the previous three years - and that before too long they would, hopefully, see the end of the war.

As Valérie tucked a tired Marianne in to bed that Christmas night, she felt hopeful. She'd been uplifted by the peaceful day the family had spent together and by the King's message. The future was uncertain, but one thing was for sure was that every day was getting closer to the end of the war. It was just that no one knew what that date was. She was grateful for the new opportunity she was going to take in the WAAF. She sensed her father's pride in her decision. And despite the hardship and difficulty of single motherhood, she was thankful for Marianne and the joy that she bought to their home.

Marianne shut her eyes and hugged Sammy close. As Valérie stroked her hair and kissed her little girl's cheek, she thought Sammy looked rather relieved after the busy day to be allowed to rest on the pillow next to Mariann.

2

Marianne

Another year had passed by with the usual investigative trips to other countries. For far too long, I'd been travelling and working away from home. It certainly wasn't all glamourous hotels and cocktails. After a while, one hotel looks much like another. I was tiring of over twenty years of business fraud investigating within the financial services sector. Each case, country and hotel room were all blending into one. And room service menus never lived up to their creative descriptions of the ingredients. I still smile at the thought of being offered a chicken Caesar salad without chicken as a vegetarian option in an upmarket Swiss establishment last year. That was probably the beginning of the end.

It had been another exhausting month travelling back and forth to Madrid, preparing the fraud case for the bank. This one had been complex. The trail of information and the meticulous detail of the evidence we needed to organise for the lawyers to present to the court had been overwhelming. I was weary after months of sifting and coordinating the paperwork confirming the tens of millions of European currency fraud. The intricate web of lies and deceit had unravelled before my eyes as I pulled the first few threads of it from the UK office. Then it had extended into Spain and Italy. The tedious dealings with all the self-important key players involved had been exhausting. But hopefully it would all be worthwhile if we could secure the conviction. Heaven knows the lawyers were charging enough for their services. Every transaction leaves a trail and by sticking to that simple rule I had followed it to its despicable destination. The murky world of money laundering. The fraudsters had turned dirty money, usually from crime, into clean funds by washing it through the legitimate banking system.

I was ready to go home and stay there for a while. Worrying about grandma was occupying more and more of my thoughts and my time. More so since Mrs Langdon, the nursing home manager, had rung me two weeks before to say that she thought, although she wasn't certain, that Winnie was becoming a little confused. And that she kept asking for me.

We would pass the evidence to the lawyers, and from there my deputy could handle things. Anyway, it would give him an opportunity to fly solo and handle the case liaison during my two-week break. I was sure he was competent; a trial run would tell me for sure before my impending early retirement at the end of the year.

And so, boarding the late afternoon flight to Heathrow felt like the right thing to be doing. I knew my absence from home over the last few months had taken its toll on grandma. While she hadn't directly said so, I'd heard some anxiety in her voice on our weekly calls. She seemed to recognise that her time was running out as she approached her 100th birthday. Her overall physical health was as good as expected at this stage in her life. But it pained me to hear her say how she was "tired in her heart", how she knew that "her time was nearly up." In her words that "the heavenly bingo caller was about to call her number". She had a certainty about being reunited with my mum, her beloved Valérie, and my grandpa Phillipe. I kept telling her not to be so morbid, she wasn't going anywhere. Well, not just yet anyway.

The flight took off at the scheduled time for a change. I relaxed into my seat, excited and longing to see grandma again. Going home felt good. I had a week to organise her special birthday party at her nursing home. She had already given me several lists, some amendments to lists and some further unreasonable requests. I was looking forward to making the best arrangements I could for the happiest of celebrations with her.

As the plane droned on through the early evening clouds, the endless stream of announcements by the cabin crew threatened to invade my brain. I closed my eyes to switch off. Tomorrows first task was to chase up family and friends for replies to the party invitations. The family's capability of being both infuriating and marvellous at the same time never ceased to amaze me.

The thought of family cast a shadow of sadness over me. A feeling of sorrow that mum wasn't here to see her own mother celebrate 100 years of life. The difference in years lived between the two women struck me: my mother's life tragically cut short at twenty-five. Yet my grandma had enjoyed an extra quarter of a century on top of her allotted 'three score and ten', as her biblical reference called them. The gulf between my two closest female relatives and their years of living seemed so unfair. But as they say, 'life isn't fair.' They also say that 'all is fair in love and war' but I'd never quite worked out whether that was true.

"Excuse me? Would you like any drinks or snacks from the trolley? We'll be landing in an hour and you've slept for most of the flight madam, I didn't want you to miss out."

The flawlessly made up young cabin crew interrupted my reverie. Her thoughtfulness touched me.

"No, but thank you for thinking of me, Anna," I said as I glanced at her name badge.

My thoughts of a missing mother had overwhelmed the last hour. As they had for many hours over my lifetime.

3

Marianne

Two weeks later

"Oh, for heaven's sake David, we're going to be late if this traffic doesn't get a move on!"

I knew it wasn't Cousin David's fault that the M1 had ground to a halt on that Saturday lunchtime. He was the closest to me and had to withstand my frustration.

"We won't make it for 3 o'clock at this rate and I don't want grandma upset and confused if we're not there for her birthday tea... we can't be late... is there another route we could go?"

My rising panic and irritability wasn't being hidden very well.

"Don't panic, no she won't Marianne," replied David. He was as practical as ever and completely ignoring my question about an alternative route. My cousin was the nearest thing to a brother I had, and he knew how to put up with me.

He started the engine again and changed up into first gear, edging the car forward a few yards into the outside lane. Then we stopped, again.

"But talk to her about 50 years ago and about stuff during the war and you'll not shut her up. I suppose that's what Dementia does to you." He spoke to the windscreen without looking at me.

David thought his Aunt Winnie was going dotty as she was getting older; I knew life exhausted her.

"Mmm... it's an awful disease and seems to affect her memories, poor thing. She's getting people mixed up, who is who, and who is dead. Don't worry if she calls you by someone else's name, David. Are you ok in the back there Aunt Ethel?"

"Yes, I'm fine. It'll be lovely to see Winnie again."

An hour later he clicked the indicator and turned left off the country lane. A large, rectangular midnight blue and gold painted sign at the roadside proclaimed all rooms enjoyed an en suite bathroom and communal kitchen. He parked the silver BMW in the tidy grounds of Longueville Private Residential Care Home. The grass had been freshly mown that morning. The immaculate flower beds planted with an array of coloured pansies.

We had made it to grandma's birthday party celebrations, only 10 minutes late after all.

The staff had dressed the sage green communal dining room with balloons, banners and birthday cards. There was a riot of colour, a steady hum of activity, and a general air of celebration in the room. The care team of busy carers helped the residents to comfy seats, poured tea and offered sandwiches and cakes around. And amid all this busyness was my grandma, sitting serenely in her new powder blue dress and matching jacket, wearing the corsage of freesias that she had been insistent on having for the occasion. There were fresh flower arrangements sitting on white linen tablecloths on every table, just as she had specified. She was having none of this plastic table covering and artificial flowers nonsense on her special day, she'd said. And the local florist must deliver fresh flowers that morning, definitely not the evening before.

I kissed her tenderly on the cheek, noticing that she, or someone, had applied some make-up to her face. Someone had washed and set her hair too. Was she really 100 years old today? Her eyes danced over the surrounding scene. She looked radiant.

"I'm sorry that we're late grandma, the traffic was awful. Happy Birthday to my favourite person." I smiled at her, calling her by my childhood term of endearment. She laughed.

"Happy birthday, Aunt Winnie," David echoed behind me. "Don't forget that you promised to dance with me first."

Her blue-grey eyes sparkled as she laughed again. As they did when she cried, I thought.

"You're here now, that's all that matters. Now get yourselves a cup of tea sorted out and you young people can help me celebrate, I'm surrounded by all these old people all day."

"Grandma!" I chided her.

Half an hour later the tinkle of a knife on a glass and a wave of 'shushing' and 'quiet' worked its way around the room.

"Good afternoon ladies and gentlemen... shhh... quiet please... right, first let me say what an absolute pleasure and a privilege it is for us all to be here with Winnie to help her celebrate her remarkable birthday." Mrs Langdon, the ever efficient home manager, stood in the middle of the dining room.

"What's that she's saying?" shouted an old gentleman seated opposite grandma, wearing all his war medals proudly on his chest.

"Ernie, please turn your hearing aid on. Could someone help him with it, please?" Mrs Langdon issued her instruction and then turned to Winnie.

Relative silence descended, which was then interrupted by a rattling noise as someone's shaky hand replaced a teacup on a saucer. Mrs Langdon crossed the room in far too few strides for an average height person. Within seconds, she was at grandma's side.

"And now it gives me even greater pleasure and honour to present our lovely Winnie here with a rather special envelope from Buckingham Palace."

Applause broke out around the room. Grandma reached out her gnarled, aged spotted hand and gently took the vellum coloured envelope from her.

"Thank you," she whispered. To me the whisper had a familiar echo, a sound from the past. She held out her other hand to me. "Marianne, I could not have gone on without you."

She carefully opened the envelope with a silver paperknife and removed its contents. As she read the greeting, grandma looked up at me. Her face crumpled inwards as she stared ahead. Silently she mouthed to me the words: "Another telegram."

As I observed her face in the crowded room, I could see the reflection of my memory of a telegram, many years ago, in her eyes too. Only I knew her thoughts at this moment. A moment in which we were just the two of us again in that cold sitting room.

"And so, as is appropriate on these occasions, especially when you have reached the remarkable age of 100, I think we should have a rousing chorus of Happy Birthday for Winnie. Stan–would you like to lead us with your rather fine baritone voice please? And Elsie has volunteered to play the piano for us."

Mrs Langdon's instruction to Stan interrupted grandma's thoughts. She too had visited the same distant place as me, one that was long ago.

After a fine tea, followed by overly sweet birthday cake, she leaned heavily on me on her left and on her stick on her right as I took her to her room. She was tired. I helped her undress and made her comfortable.

"Oh, thank you for a wonderful day Marianne, it has been perfect. Now come and sit with me... I need to talk to you... I need to give you something."

"Grandma, it can wait until tomorrow. I'm coming back to pick you up and take you out for lunch. Remember?"

"No, you need to take it with you now, so that I don't forget... it's important... I don't want someone throwing away my treasure, they'll think it's junk when I'm gone. I need to know that you have it and it's safe."

What treasure was she talking about? I did not know what she meant.

"Would you hang my dress up in the wardrobe dear, then look on the second shelf down, right at the back... there's a red tin, it's for you."

I retrieved an old biscuit tin from the shelf. The tin had lived a life with faded red paint, the edges of the lid worn smooth by years of use. It had a dent on one side. I had a hazy memory of seeing this tin as a young child.

Sitting on the bed, I placed it between us. Grandma looked at me with tender tears in her eyes.

"This is my treasure, my collection of dear and special things, and I want you to have them because they rightly belong to you. Promise me you'll look after them and treasure them too... they will tell you something about your mother, about my Valérie."

I laughed at the unlikely prospect of the ageing old tin containing anything of any value or a priceless artefact.

"Of course I'll take care of it."

"Oh Marianne, I always tried to do my best for you and look after you, even though it was difficult for me... you always reminded me of her. You have her strength."

"Please don't fret Grandma, it was good enough for me. But it still makes me sad to think that I never knew her properly... not really, not as a person... her likes and dislikes and so on... so thank you for keeping the things in the tin for me... whatever they are."

"Please promise me you'll keep it safe and read the bits and pieces I've kept about her. They are yours and will tell you about her... now you have some time to yourself... did you tell me you are not working now? I can't remember... I'm sorry Marianne, my memories are getting jumbled up. I am tired."

I hated to see her agitated like this. So kissing her, I removed the tin from the bed and placed it next to my handbag.

"Of course, I promise. We can talk about your treasure tomorrow. Now let's get you comfortable... it's been a big day for you. Hasn't it been lovely, though? That's right, you snuggle down, I'll leave the small lamp on while you read for a while. I just need to pop along to Mrs Langdon's office and thank her properly for her help today."

When I returned, I found her asleep. Her book and her glasses resting on her chest, rising and falling as her gentle breathing became heavier. Dimming the lamp, I sat on the sofa and quietly loosened the lid of the battered biscuit tin. As I lifted the layers of letters, postcards and photographs with precious and sentimental value to grandma, I could see nothing of great value there. Replacing the items, an old, black and white photograph slid from the pile. It floated down to the blue carpet. I picked it up and squinted in the half light of the dimly lit room. An old photograph of a couple. The woman was my mother, but she was with a man I did not recognise. They were smiling at the camera. I had never seen this photograph of her before.

I carefully replaced the image on top of the contents in the tin and replaced the lid. As I walked out to the car park, where David was patiently waiting, I made a mental note to ask grandma tomorrow about the man in the picture. Who was he?

"You ok Marianne? You look tired, it's been a big day," he said as I placed my handbag and the tin on the back seat of the car next to Aunt Ethel.

4

Marianne

The telegram autumn 1943

I was about four years old on the day it happened. I recall some events with absolute clarity. Others have faded as time has weathered them: like the cliffs being eroded by the sea, time has worn the edges away.

That day there was a loud knock on our green front door that sounded different somehow: urgent and loud. A knock at a front door sometimes sounds like that.

Grandma Winnie frowned as she glanced up from the kitchen bench to the clock on the wall. It was 11.06am on a bright September Monday morning. She hadn't been expecting anyone. Well possibly, she might have a visit from Jim the Air Raid Protections Warden. She knew she'd allowed a chink of light to escape through the blackout curtain over the back door in the previous night's air raid. To slip out to the privy at the end of the yard was risky: opening the door and then venturing out while she could hear the German bombers overhead. But she'd been desperate for our outside toilet. She said she would not allow this wretched war to rob her of her pride and self-respect. She would not use a bucket, as many of our neighbours did.

Grandma had made a cake on the day it happened. It was a pale yellow sponge cake. She'd said she'd put some watery homemade strawberry jam in the middle of it later. And I could have a tea party with my rag doll, Sammy.

There was a sweet smell of baking, and it warmed the kitchen for us. Even now, the aroma of homemade cake reminds me of that day. She had just eased the springy warm sponge out of its tin on to the wire rack to cool. I can see her wiping her hands on the already-wet tea towel, checking her hair in the small round mirror hanging by a piece of string to the left of the sink. She smoothed down her pinafore.

"Marianne, stay there and play with Sammy while I answer the front door to Jim. If I have to defend myself and take a telling off from him, then I want to look presentable. Anyway, it's probably only what I deserve." Grandma reflected on her foolishness, but then reasoned with herself that needs must, even in wartime.

Peeping out from the upturned chairs with an old blanket spread across the top that was a pretend air raid shelter, I looked for the source of the interruption to my imaginary world. A blue eyed little girl playing in front of the fireless grate, I glanced up from under my mousy coloured fringe. "Yes, Grandma," and then returned to playing shops with my building blocks.

Although grandma was average height, I noticed she stood up tall, put on her best, most friendly smile and walked purposefully down the thinning brown carpet of the hallway to the front door. Perhaps Jim might not be so hard on her if invited in for a cup of tea and a slice of the small but precious cake. She'd saved up rations of sugar and flour. "A cup of tea made everything feel better." She often said that.

I remember the squeaky creak as she opened the door; the top hinge still needed some oil on it.

"Oh, hello, can I help you?"

But it wasn't Jim at the front step of our modest but neat semi in north London. Grandmas stature was only temporary. Her shoulders sank. I saw her visibly shrink as alarm rose within her. I'd peeped through the gap in the kitchen door to see a man in a uniform. As a child, I told people it was a soldier standing there. Years later she told me it filled her with terror when she saw the blue-grey Royal Air Force uniform of a youngish man, of officer rank there. He respectfully held his hat in front of him with both hands, but as he moved it from his right hand to his left, I noticed the telegram. Grandma knew it was the angel of death visiting. His left hand clutched it tightly. I remember the whites of his knuckles.

"Mrs Bouchard? May I come in? I am Captain Fawcett."

The voice spoke with authority and gentleness. The officer took a step forward and invited himself into our house. Grandma was silent. She stared at him and opened the front sitting room door. How odd, we didn't use 'the best room' very often. It was cold in there without a fire. Many years later, she told me she had a feeling that one day we might play this scenario out.

"Oh, yes, please, come in, where are my manners?... please, sit down, in here... I'm sorry there's no fire in the grate; can I get you some tea? You know coal is so scarce these days. But I have some sugar left."

The mixed up words all tumbled out of her mouth at once. They made no sense to me as she was saying them. Grandma's usual calm manner had disappeared, and I felt anxious. What was happening? She rarely talked quickly like that. She had turned into a different person.

"No, but thank you, Mrs Bouchard. You must save your precious sugar for your family. And there is absolutely no need to apologise for the national lack of coal."

A soft half smile did not reach his eyes. He sat down on the worn sofa and asked himself whether he would ever get used to delivering terrible news to ordinary families. Some ranking officers may not see active service like others, but we have other dreadful things to endure, he thought.

"Is Mr Bouchard in? Could you ask him to join us, please?"

"I'm afraid that there is only my granddaughter Marianne and me in the house now. Phillipe is dead, he died in January... in the air raid on Weston Street... the one that killed our neighbours son John... he was home on leave for a weekend, they were just doing their fire duty... but I know that's not why you're here..."

The words tumbled from her mouth again. I recall her voice became quieter as she spoke. To Captain Fawcett, her words tapered off and then evaporated into a whisper.

"I am so very sorry Mrs Bouchard, I think you should sit down, I have some sad news about Valérie," said Captain Fawcett. He tentatively handed her the telegram.

Grandma stood perfectly still, as though frozen, looking at it. Then her knees weakened as she sat heavily in the brown armchair to the right of the fire grate. It had been my grandpa Phillipe's chair. She tried to steady her shaking hand as she took the cream coloured piece of paper from his manicured hand. She said nothing. The words, unspoken, stuck in her throat. But she knew her feeling of foreboding had been correct. It was indeed bad news.

The bitter words of the telegram that delivered the news of my mum's death merged before her blue silver-grey eyes. The words were brief, to the point. They did not portray her daughter's colourful and infectious love of life. They were black, cold and stark words. She refolded the piece of paper in her trembling hands and struggled to blink back the tears in front of this stranger.

I heard their voices and then it went deathly silent in the other room. I felt frightened. The air felt still. I stood as quietly as I could in the hallway. The fourth floorboard along had a squeak, so I'd stepped over it. Little did I know then that death caused the silence. The sitting room door was ajar. Grandma opened her mouth, but I couldn't hear what she said as her voice went quieter than a whisper. Then it disappeared.

I knew she had caught my movement in the corner of her left eye. I stood in the doorway, cradling my one-eyed rag doll Sammy.

"Grandma, what's happened to Mummy?"

Her face was pale, yet she had been rosy cheeked when she'd left the warm kitchen.

"Grandma, your eyes are wet, I'll make it better."

I panicked. I couldn't remember seeing grandma cry before. Did grown-ups cry? In my young childhood innocence, I thought only children had tears when they fell over and cut their knee or banged their head. It was cold in the room. She shivered. I didn't think it was because we didn't have a fire going.

I never forgot the look on the man's face as I edged around the door into the room. I should not have been listening. I thought I would get into trouble. But grandma had suddenly shrunk within her body, a broken shell on the edge of the armchair. I don't know how I knew I had to make her feel better. I climbed up into her lap and hugged her. The once safe, warm hiding place for me now felt empty and cold. Grandma's small hands felt as though they were ice covered. Her face was ashen.

Captain Fawcett cleared his throat as he slowly stood up, feeling as though his heart was breaking for this poor woman and child who had made many sacrifices for the war effort. First her beloved husband and now her only child, her daughter, who had so plainly been courageous in leaving her own daughter in the care of her grandparents.

"I will take my leave of you now, Mrs Bouchard. Please accept the sincerity of the condolences of the War Office and the King, to which I add my own. I cannot imagine your loss, but please take comfort from the fact that your daughter died an honourable death serving her country. We shall be forever indebted to her and..." His voice trailed off, lost for words. "I'll let myself out, please make yourself that cup of tea and get warm."

I did not understand the words that he said about the King. Was he here? Was he waiting outside our house for the stranger in our sitting room? The man in the blue uniform bowed towards grandma and me. He picked up his hat. I saw it had a winged badge on the front of it. As he left the room, he stroked the top of my head. His hand was icy too.

I heard the front door softly close as grandma picked me up and carried me through to the back kitchen. I sat down on the mat. She filled the kettle and lit the stove, rubbing her hands together over the heat of the gas ring. She put the freshly baked cake in an old and dented Crawfords Shortbread biscuit tin. There was no slice of cake to accompany this cup of tea. She was still crying.

Grandma allowed me in her enormous bed on the night of the day it happened. Cuddling Sammy, I worked out that it wasn't the King who was dead. I was unsure whether he had been waiting outside for our visitor, though. The world can be very confusing for a child. But I had a knowing, a child's certainty that my world had changed forever. I just wasn't sure how. As the weeks and months passed, I suppose everyone thought I was too young to understand what had happened. And so, no one ever really told me that my mother wasn't coming back. She was missing.

5

Marianne

Memories

Grandma died a week after her 100th birthday. I took the call as I waited in the baggage reclaim hall of the terminal at Heathrow. The unfamiliar ring tone of my new-fangled Nokia mobile phone echoed around the hall. It joined a growing chorus as holidaymakers and business types alike switched their mobiles back on after the flight.

"She went so peacefully Marianne, she wasn't in any pain... she said she was so exhausted. She said to tell you she loved you and to give you a message."

"Oh, Mrs Langdon... I've just landed back in the UK and was coming straight up to see her."

"My dear, don't worry about coming now, we'll sort out the arrangements, the doctor is on his way."

"No, I want to be with her, I'll be there in a couple of hours, depends how quickly I get through Customs. It seems to take far longer than it used to."

"Ok, we'll see you when you get here. Would you like us to make you a sandwich or anything?"

"That's very kind of you, but there's no need to bother."

"One other thing, Marianne... could I ask whether Winnie made her wishes known to you about funeral arrangements? It'd be surprising if she hadn't."

I could feel Mrs Langdon's care over the phone. "I know it's a delicate subject, but I could give the undertakers a call for you."

"Oh, thank you, Mrs Langdon, that's truly kind of you. Would you? It would be an immense help, please. Yes, she has her funeral arrangements all planned out. Typical grandma, eh? It's Richards and Howard in the old town, in Queen Street, I think."

"Yes, they are, they're an excellent company. I'll give Mr Richards a call, actually he's a friend of mine. A very courteous man, I'll make sure they take good care of Winnie for you."

"Thank you, Mrs Langdon... I really appreciate it."

"Please Marianne, I've told you before–call me Sally."

"Thank you, Sally."

As I replaced the phone in my handbag I saw the scribbled note to myself on the flight and put in the red-lined side pocket:

Ask Grandma about the photo in the tin.

I had forgotten to ask her who the man in the photograph was over the previous weekend amidst the happiness of her birthday celebrations. And now it was too late.

As I drove from the airport to grandmas nursing home, the motorway miles passed by in a blur as the shock of the news touched me. A deep sadness at not being with her in the end engulfed me. I should have been there to hold her hand. I felt I had let her down: the feeling of always needing to protect grandma surfaced again.

Long-forgotten scenes entered my head as they lost me in childhood memories of her, and by association, my mum.

They say that children can be cruel. That was true of some things I remember in my childhood. I can't remember quite what triggered it, but as usual my classmates made me cry. Perhaps it was the feeling that I wasn't like them. I was different. Having to explain, yet again, that no, I didn't have a mum, and yes, she'd died when she was away doing war work. And yes, I lived with my grandmother. It didn't occur to me, not at first, that other children didn't live like we did. Grandma and me, our own little family.

The war was a great leveller in some ways, we'd all had more or less next to nothing as the Government tried to share things out equally with the rationing system. But what had bound many families together were the missing fathers, brothers, husbands, cousins who were away fighting.

My memory of my school years was that my world was different though. Mine had a missing mother and my absent male relatives. Grandpa Phillipe had died, and I didn't know who my father was. There was only my Aunt Ethels son, my Uncle Martin, and his son, my cousin, David. He was two years older than me and wasn't interested in playing with an annoying younger girl cousin when grandma asked him to.

The classroom was a relatively safe place. There I immersed myself, learning about the world then and in times gone by. I escaped into the colourful and moving world of words in books and writing. But understanding numbers I always found more difficult. They were too static, regimented, and black on the page. Now I smiled to myself. The irony of applying myself over the years to understanding digits and then working in the financial fraud world had not escaped me.

The safety of the classroom, under the teacher's control by her watchful eyes, was where my classmates couldn't taunt me. The feeling of being cocooned between the wooden chair and the desk was a comfort. But the playground had been a unique environment – often openly hostile and threatening as the other children taunted me and called me names. And then, of course, they denied it when the teacher tried to reprimand them for my tears.

I think it was a usual Tuesday, and I thought that I'd got through the day unscathed when they quietly followed me towards the school gates and gathered around me. The feeling of their presence and proximity was familiar – a brooding intent to upset me, just because they could. It would take the same course each time: like a trickle of water on dry ground, their hurtful comments would find their way to the saddest spot in my soul. I longed to be the same as them and join in with them so that my life mingled with theirs.

"Are you going home, Marianne? Isn't anyone meeting you to take you home?"

"Why isn't your Mum coming to fetch you from school?"

All the usual questions... led by the same ringleader—Flo Jackson, with her pretty blond curls—and the others like fish in a pond or sheep in the field, just following her, meekly, blindly, not realising the consequences of their actions or their words. And then there's Dorothy, who calls herself my friend, on the edge of the group, not quite in but not out either. When we were just the two of us, she's different. I think she likes to be everyone's friends and won't say no to Flo.

"No, I'm allowed to walk home by myself," I'd reply confidently with my voice, but with an internal bravery I didn't feel in my body. Shaking, I'd just keep walking.

"My Mum said it just wasn't right that your Mum went away to do war work. She said it's not right that a mother should go away and just leave her child, not during a war or anytime, she could have done some closer to home... she says that war work is man's work, anyway."

Flo's voice was the intended well-aimed arrow and hit its target. It pierced the space between my shoulder blades.

"Well, my Mum says that it wasn't right that she didn't have a husband either... and it's not fair that it left your grandmother to bring you up."

The pain of their vicious words went deep into my soul. Dorothy's voice rattled in my head as I ran along the street and turned the corner so that they wouldn't see my tears. If I cried too hard or for too long, then grandma would guess when she saw my red eyes, and I didn't want her to have her sad face. I knew she was sad enough in her heart.

And so, I would often take a retreat into my own fanciful world: another realm where I could imagine myself as another girl, growing up with a normal life, instead of being different. I imagined, no - I became a girl who had an ordinary name like Susan or something similar, not some foreign, exotic French name. What kind of name was Marianne, anyway? One that gave my classmates a good reason to make fun of me, that's what. In my make-believe life, I had two parents like ordinary children in my class, and we lived a proper family life.

Of course I didn't dare tell grandma about this world I went to; I instinctively knew that she would have slipped into her sad face and her watery eyes if I had. And so, feeling the responsibility for her happiness, I kept it to myself, my daydream world of imagining things that did not exist. But the make-believe world was real to me.

I couldn't tell her about any of this, as I knew it would break her heart. I had overheard one of our neighbours say that one woman in our street had died from a broken heart when she had received the telegram to say her husband had died fighting. In my young mind, something unknown connected the two things and terrified me. We had received a telegram and grandma was still alive: but for how long?

As time passed, I worked out that it must be something to do with how sad you were about the telegram that must kill you. And grandma always seemed to be cheerful, so that must keep her alive. And so I could not risk making her any sadder with my inner thoughts. What would happen to me if she went away too? Where would I go? Who would look after me? And so my daily task was also my biggest fear. The conundrum of how to keep grandma alive by not making her sad and upset.

6

Marianne

Winnies funeral

It was a bright yellow sunshine day as the mourners slowly walked toward the black hearse and their cars after the service at the crematorium. The gathering hadn't been large - how many friends are still with you when you've turned 100 years of age; I pondered. Her sister Aunt Ethel and a few younger family members, staff from the nursing home, the ever attentive Sally Langdon. And Janet, my next door neighbour. But no friends from her life, I thought with sadness.

My heart was empty yet fluttery as I passed through the rusty iron gate into the garden of remembrance. The undertaker had gathered together in a corner the skilfully prepared multi coloured arrangements from family and friends. The riot of colour felt offensive against the backdrop of my dark sadness. And yet the thought of people's kindness made me smile briefly as I knelt to pick up the message cards and read them.

One exquisitely arranged blue iris and red and white rose posy caught my eye. The thick message card had script handwriting. It was antique-looking, with curled letters and flourishes. It read:

For my dearest Winnie,

I will never forget your sacrifice during the war and have felt your loss with you through the years.

My wish and prayer are for you to be reunited with Valérie,

With respectful wishes,

Jacques.

The words perplexed me. Who on earth was Jacques? Grandma had never mentioned him to me. And what sacrifice had she made? Who else felt mum's loss like grandma and me? Just how did this person know my mum had died? So many questions were swirling around in my thoughts. They did not have answers.

Replacing the card into the flowers, I saw a tall, ageing yet distinguished looking gentleman approaching me. His outstanding quality woollen overcoat was buttoned up, an immaculately tied wine-red scarf peeped through the collar. He finished the look with a gentle smile.

He held his long fingered right hand out to me, looked directly into my eyes and spoke in a soft French accent.

"My dear Marianne, it is a pleasure to meet you at last. I had to come and pay my respects to Winnie. France and I honour her and owed her a debt of gratitude for what Valérie did for us and for the sacrifice Winnie gave."

His words confused me. This was grandma's funeral, not my mothers. I looked at the man in astonishment and steadied myself. My legs felt weak as I tried to compose my haphazard thoughts. Mention of mum had caught me off guard. Who was this stranger?

"Please, excuse my ignorance, but were you a friend of Winnies? I don't recall that we have met before."

"No, please forgive me, I knew your mother during the war, we served together, we served our countries."

"Oh... I see."

But I didn't see at all. I did not know who this man was.

"Marianne, this is a sad day and I do not wish to take any more of your time. I felt I had to pay my respects. Au revoir."

"But-"

He graciously bowed and kissed my hand then briskly walked away towards a waiting car; its rear door being held open by a dark suited chauffeur complete with peaked cap.

I stared after him. Who was this man? He knew my mother and disconcertingly, this stranger knew my name. But how? He had not given me his name. I went to follow him, but I could not ask my questions as someone called my name. I turned to hear the loud sobbing from my now extremely frail Aunt Ethel approaching me.

"Now then Aunt Ethel, don't upset yourself, grandma would hate to see you so upset... come on now, is Uncle Martin or David going to take you home?"

As I looked up, the car was leaving the crematorium grounds. I could not make out the registration plate.

The empathetic Mr Richards, the Funeral Director, stepped silently into the garden and gently appeared at my side.

"Are you ok Marianne? Ready to go now?"

"Yes, I think so. Do you know who the elderly gentleman was? Did he send flowers?"

"No, I'm afraid I don't know who that was."

"Would you... could you collect the message cards from the floral tributes for me, Mr Richards?"

"Of course, give me a few minutes and I'll be with you."

I turned my face to the sunshine and couldn't help but think that grandma would have loved her send off with her favourite music and poems.

"Aah, there you are, Marianne. I'm going to go on ahead and put the kettle on and set out the buffet for those who are coming back to the house. Do you think there'll be many?" Janet, my neighbour stood close to me with her hand on my arm.

"Janet, you're an absolute star, thank you. No - I don't think there'll be that many to be honest, Aunt Ethel and David definitely, and some staff from the nursing home, you and me... thank you. "

She hugged me and off she went as Mr Richards gently took my arm and guided me back to the sleek, panther-like black funeral car. He handed me the condolence cards from the flowers and I slipped them into my coat pocket.

That evening after the family gathering for sandwiches, tea, and small talk in the summer room, I was glad to be alone in silence. I wrote a note on the kitchen to do list: I must properly thank Janet tomorrow for clearing the dishes and washing up.

But now it was time for bed, and suddenly, I felt bone and brain weary. I undressed and hung up my black dress and coat in the recently fitted new wardrobes. I removed the message cards from the silk-lined coat pocket before the glass-fronted door closed silently.

I sat on my bed, thinking that I must thank friends and family for sending flowers and making donations to grandmas chosen charity. One card was thicker that the others and I turned this one over in my fingers. Who was this man, Jacques? How was he connected to my family?

Feeling emotional, lost, and exhausted, I placed the cards on the bed-side table next to the silver framed photos of grandma and mum. I blew them both a kiss as I pulled back the covers, got into bed and hugged myself. Eventually I fell into a fitful sleep.

7

Valérie

May 1943

Valérie hurried that May morning. She had overslept again. Marianne had woken twice during the night with disturbed dreams. The war was affecting every generation. The lack of restful sleep was another shortage, a rare commodity unavailable on the black market. She couldn't be late on duty to relieve the night shift. Her Women's Air Auxiliary Forces colleagues, the WAAF for short, would be weary from their intense concentration of tracking the approaching German bombers. As she rounded the corner, it was a relief to see her usual travelling companions at the bus stop, still waiting in a line against the Co-op store wall.

She joined the back of the queue, facing the early morning sunshine, enjoying the renewing heat as time headed towards summer. The brightness momentarily lifted her spirits and shut out the grey grimness of this seemingly endless war. Tomorrow her rota would change again to night shifts, back to listening out for messages about the unpredictable air raids that caused the blackness in the streets and the fear in people's hearts. Valérie closed her eyes, remembering quieter and more peaceful, warm summer days pushing Marianne in her pram in the park.

The mechanical sound of the approaching vehicle roused her from the memory. Disappointingly it was the no.57, her bus was now five minutes late. The green bus pulled away, and it left the WAAF girls waiting. Valérie listened to the usual chatter of the trading of stockings, cigarettes, and gossip. The rumours she overheard made her smile. Apparently someone knew someone who had a friend who could get them some lipstick. For a price, of course.

She heard footsteps behind her as someone joined the queue. She looked over her shoulder but didn't recognise the man in uniform.

"Excuse me, but may I trouble you for a light, please?" asked the well-spoken man.

Valérie turned around to face the tall man in officer rank RAF uniform.

"I'm afraid I don't smoke Sir, but Celia does, two people down the line."

The man took a couple of confident strides forward, then returned to his place in the queue with his lighted cigarette. She heard him take a deep inhale and blow out the smoke. Valérie coughed as she breathed in the used nicotine that wafted across her shoulder.

"Oh, please forgive me Valérie, I apologise, that's awfully rude of me." The look on his face was apologetic, a little like a scolded child.

Valérie was unnerved. How did this stranger, obviously an officer, know her name?

"Have we met before... Sir?"

"No, we haven't."

He took a long drag on his cigarette and exhaled the smoke in the opposite direction.

Valérie stared at the man as he continued to smoke his cigarette. He consumed the tobacco and dropped the smoking remains to the floor. Then, with his polished right black leather shoe, he moved his foot from left to right, grinding the remains into the pavement.

"May I ask Sir – how do you know my name?"

"Yes, of course, my apologies – again. I should have introduced myself."

Valérie looked behind him. "I'll have to go now Sir, the bus is coming Sir."

The unnamed man stood up straight and said, "Please do not worry about your shift and do not get on the bus with the others. It will probably raise a few eyebrows, but that's of no consequence." This was an order and delivered in a tone that came naturally to him. It was not a request.

"It may be of no consequence to you, Sir, but I have to work as I have a child...."

The man put his hand on her arm and shook his head as the bus stopped at the flaking green painted metal bus stop. Valérie was in a quandary. If she didn't catch the bus, her colleagues would be on a short staffed shift and wouldn't get a tea break, but if she disobeyed orders from a senior ranked officer, then she would face a disciplinary appointment with the air base commanding officer.

Celia turned in the queue, "Valérie come on, never mind chatting with a handsome fella - we're late as it is. The driver won't wait, y'know what he's like when he's behind schedule."

"Cover for me Celia, will you? Tell the Captain that I missed the bus... I'll be there as soon as I can, I have to do something first."

"I bet you do," came Celia's raucous laugh.

The no.49 pulled away from the bus stop without her as Celia waved from the backseat window.

The man had a wry smile on his face as she turned to him.

"I'm sorry to have put you in that situation... Now Valérie, I must speak with you about an important matter... in private if we may... I believe that there is a park around the corner." Again the tone of his voice was an order, not a polite request, as he took her elbow and guided her forward.

After a few minutes, they entered the park. He pointed to a bench. She sat down. He remained standing and pulled another cigarette from his uniform jacket pocket, lit it and inhaled deeply. The exhaled smoke evaporated into the late spring day.

"Valérie, please listen carefully to what I have to say to you: this is a matter of national importance. They have informed me that your translations are extremely accurate and I hear you speak fluent French, is that correct?"

"Yes... Sir," she replied hesitantly. Just how did this stranger know so much about her?

"Your skills have not gone unnoticed in the listening room, and there are certain divisions within the War department that need people of your ability."

"Oh, thank you... but there are other girls there who can speak French."

"I'm told your attention to details is impressive and also the manner in which you speak French, not with an obviously English accent."

Valérie was unsure what her response should be. She felt unnerved that she was being watched and listened to while doing her bit for her country.

"My Father was French but I have a feeling that you already know that Sir. So just how is this a matter of national security, Sir? I have broken no rules or told anyone about what I hear and translate... I don't understand."

"Please don't worry about it at the moment, we will explain more when you come to London. It is imperative that you tell no one – not your friends nor your family about this conversation. Tomorrow morning we will collect you at 8.00am prompt outside the park gates. You will catch the train into London, please be ready; they will meet you at Euston, a driver, I think. And we will brief you when you arrive at our office."

"But I must go in for my shift tomorrow Sir, I will be on night shift... and I'm already late today, and that's just not fair on the other girls."

"Marianne, listen to me, this is all arranged - your shift leader knows of your absence because of illness. Now, you are to return home to your family and enjoy a day with them. Tell them you were unwell, and you have returned home. And please, follow your orders for tomorrow."

"But I'm not ill."

"Valérie, please do not fret, it is all taken care of. We need people like you to help us. This could help us win the war."

And with that the unnamed man raised his hand to his cap, saluted her and walked away.

8

Marianne

The next day

It was 3.36am when the bedside clock blinked at me. I was unsure what had woken me. I listened: it wasn't a noise inside or outside the house. The hush of the early morning spoke its own language of new beginnings. I closed my eyes again. I could still see the blurred image of the photograph in my dream. Feeling muffled with sleep, I couldn't quite recall where I had seen this scene. I tried to settle down to sleep again, but it was useless.

Half an hour later I was filling the kettle. Dawn wouldn't break for a while over the fields. My cat, Aslan, stirred briefly on his bed, opened one eye to dismiss me as the disturbance to his sleep, then curled up again to resume his slumber.

A dawning of a different kind encroached into my thoughts. The image, a blurred photograph in my dream. I switched the quiet boil kettle on, went to the dresser and picked up grandma's old red Crawfords biscuit tin that held her papers and photos. Had it really only been four weeks ago since she had given me the tin? We had laughed together when she had said that it contained 'her treasure' And now, as I removed the stiff lid again, the black and white photograph of a couple smiled back at me... a young dark-haired man held the woman in the photograph close to him. The woman was my mother.

I stared at the photograph for what felt like an eternity, yet it couldn't have been as the kettle started its soft whistle. Placing the picture gently on the worktop, I filled the china teapot and removed a cup and saucer from the dresser shelf. One of my earliest childhood memories was of grandma's insistence that while we may not have been rich, we could have standards and some finer things in life. To her this meant tea made 'properly' as she called it, in a teapot and served in a cup and saucer. The move to tea bags in a mug in more recent times had horrified her. The thought of grandma's disapproving look at such a practice bought a smile to my face as I poured my first cup from the teapot. I, too, could not bring myself to accept such a practice.

The couple in the photograph continued to smile back at me as I gently placed the fine china cup into the saucer. I retrieved my glasses from the top of my head, put them on and picked up the image. The woman was definitely my mother–the dark wavy hair, the wide smile, the proud stance. She had the same demeanour in my bedside photo of her in the silver frame, taken in her WAAF uniform before she left to work at the south coast RAF station where she died. I never saw her again after that day.

But who was the gentleman with her? Smart but casually dressed in an open-necked white shirt with its sleeves turned up to his elbows, his right arm draped over my mothers' shoulder. They made a handsome couple, as grandma would have said. I squinted at the photograph. Did he bear a vague similarity to the elderly man at the funeral yesterday? I could not decide, after all it was the briefest of meetings and then he had disappeared.

I hurried upstairs to the bedroom and picked up the message card from the flowers on the bedside table. Returning to the kitchen, I poured another cup of tea and placed the card next to the photograph. Were these two items connected? But how? Why had the stranger turned up at the funeral? Why did he feel a need to pay his respects to my grandma? And how was it possible for him, if it was him, to be in a photograph with mum? There were far too many questions with no answers.

As I rose from the stool at the breakfast bar, I brushed the photograph from the tin with my fluffy dressing gown sleeve. It floated to the floor, landing face down. I knelt to pick it up and saw the handwriting on the back of it. It wasn't grandmas handwriting, which seemed odd. She had always meticulously labelled photographs, saying that they would be useless to future generations if they did not say who was in the photograph and its location.

Returning it to the marble surface, I heard a noise outside. There was a knock at the back patio door as I refilled the kettle and pressed the switch. I turned to see Janet with her usual chaotic dress sense: spotty pyjamas and an exotically patterned oriental dressing gown.

"Come in, come in flower, it's open." I beckoned her in. As she opened the door, the now awake Aslan sneaked out between her and the door frame. As usual, he was bigger than his boots and shot me a feline look of catch me if you can, I'm wild and free.

"Oh Marianne, are you ok? I got up around 5 o'clock... you know how it is with these night sweats, I'll be glad when the bloody thing is over... and I saw your kitchen light was on. You look pale, did you not sleep?"

"No, not very well... too much in my head at the moment... would you like some tea, Janet?"

"Yes please, but only if you're making some for yourself."

"I am, it's no trouble. I was going to pop in this morning anyway and thank you for all your help yesterday, I couldn't have managed without you. There was going to be flowers with my thanks, but you'll have to make do with tea at the moment."

I knew my neighbour wouldn't want the fuss of flowers. Over the years we had become good friends as Janet had looked after Aslan, the house and the garden for me while I'd travelled on business.

I placed butter and marmalade next to Janet together with a freshly made pot of tea. There was some toast under the grill.

"So... what are you planning to do today, Marianne? Shall we go for a walk by the river? We could stop and have lunch at that lovely little bistro, my treat. I think it would do you good to get some fresh air."

"I'm not sure yet... I haven't thought that far ahead, to be honest... I have some phone calls to make... some thank you cards to send, to say thank you for coming and sending flowers. But to be honest, I don't feel up to it yet... perhaps I'll do them later, sometime this week..."

I placed the toast on some striped blue and cream Cornishware plates.

"Marianne is something wrong? You don't seem to be quite with it this morning... I know it's early and you're upset; you need to take some time off and allow yourself to grieve. It's ok to not to be on top of the world... I'll miss Winnie too."

"Eat your toast while it's hot, Janet. I know - you're right and I have two weeks booked off... I still have some of grandma's things to sort out. She has, sorry I should say had... she had some lovely clothes, classic labels that I will take to the charity shop."

The hot buttered toast with the tangy orange topping tasted delicious: I realised I hadn't actually eaten since breakfast yesterday. So much had happened over the last 24 hours, and the sands of time seemed to have shifted beneath me. The funeral had invited me back to childhood memories of grandma. And now this photograph of mum. This felt as though it was leading me to an unknown place.

"Thank you, Marianne, this is really nice, not every day I get an unexpected breakfast invitation!"

"Talking of unexpected, did you see an elderly, well-dressed gentleman at the funeral yesterday? Rather distinguished looking, red scarf and with a chauffeur of all things."

"Yes, I did actually, he asked me to point you out as we left the service in the chapel. He sounded foreign, err French, I think? But well-spoken English... did he find you?"

Janet popped the last corner of her crust into her mouth and washed it down with the cup of tea.

"Yes... yes, he found me... and it was all very odd, Janet. He mentioned grandma and said that he'd known mum during the war. You could have knocked me down with a feather. The strange thing is that she never mentioned him as far as I can remember."

"A man of mystery then?"

"Well, it appears there is a mystery."

"Ooh, now that's intriguing. Did he say who he was?"

Janet place the dirty dishes in the sink and refilled the kettle again. She opened the kitchen blind and the early sunlight flooded on to the pale lemon painted kitchen walls.

"Well, that's just it - he didn't... and... look at this." I handed the photograph from the biscuit tin to Janet.

"That's your mum, isn't it? Gosh, she looks so happy. Who is the man? When was this taken?"

"Turn it over."

Janet looked up at me, just as confused as I was. The faded lettering was just about legible. It read

Lucille and Claude, Saint Girons, October 1943.

"But who is Lucille? That's Valérie... Where is Saint Girons?"

"I don't know, Janet; I've never heard of a Lucille before, it wasn't her middle name, that was Ann... but it's definitely mum."

My mind was racing with so many thoughts that were bumping into one another and falling over themselves. They would not line up neatly in a row so that I could work through them. I could not make any logical sense of them.

"And I don't know who Claude is... but I know Saint Girons is in France."

Janet glanced up from the picture at me, pure astonishment painted on her face.

"Do you think the picture could be the French stranger at the funeral? If you look closely it could be him, couldn't it? I mean when he was younger." Or was I clutching at straws?

"It might be... do you think? Whoever the photographer was taking it a long time ago means there was a third person there... oh Marianne... this is all so exciting... like something in a book or a film where a stranger turns up and has a secret."

"Don't be so dramatic Janet, of course it's not, you're letting your imagination run away with you, woman."

I smiled at her creative ability to see something more than I could– that's why Janet was a crazy haired creative artist who brought into existence amazing pictures and I was a logical, number cruncher corporate fraud investigator.

"The man who turned up yesterday said he knew my mother... if it's true, then I have to speak to him. But he didn't introduce himself– which is rather odd, don't you think? Y'know I was thinking about her last night and I didn't ever really know her properly, as a person I mean. Grandma always talked about her positively, but I'd love to have another person's perspective of her... that's if he knew her."

"So - the question is, how are you going to find him? You don't even know his full name."

"I don't know... but you know me, I'll think of something, I'm good at finding hidden information."

9

Valérie

The following day

Valérie walked her usual route towards the bus stop but turned left in the direction of the park gates. She glanced at her watch. The white dial declared it was 7.58am. She was glad she had put her military issue overcoat on and put her umbrella in her bag; the weather had turned chillier with some fine drizzle in the air. She yawned, she hadn't slept again. The unanswered questions by the nameless man had twirled around in a spiral in her mind most of the night and then just as she had drifted into slumber, the air raid siren cut into her dream.

As she waited, she wondered what the connection was between her ability to speak French and helping to win the war. Who needed this skill? Who was she going to see in London? Valérie felt exhausted and yet curious about who had been observing her. Surely it would do no harm to go up to London and listen to whatever their explanation–whoever 'they' might be. It would be a change of scene for her and she might bring Marianne and Winnie something nice back, if any of the shops had things in stock.

She looked up as she heard a car approach. Just as the officer had said, a black car arrived promptly at 8.00am.

The driver got out and opened the rear passenger door for her.

"Now Miss," said a blue uniformed man, "I've been told to give you these train tickets and tell you that there will be a car like this one waiting to collect you at Euston Station."

At the station he opened the door again for her, making Valérie feel special. She hadn't travelled in a car for a long time, and never in one with a chauffeur.

"Have a safe journey," he bid her as he tipped his cap at her.

"I will, thank you... I'm so sorry, what is your name?"

"Oh, you don't need to know that... I'm just the driver. Now go on, you'll miss your train."

"Well, thank you again."

Valérie entered the station and headed for platform one for trains to the south. Not that it was obvious which platform was which. You could not tell by looking around. The directive from the War Office had removed all signposts and public signage as a precaution and a hinderance to any invaders or spies. To make it difficult for them to travel about within the UK.

Military personnel in various uniforms of different hues milled about. A party of schoolchildren huddled together, some were crying, some had their little hands held a little too tightly by their sobbing and worried looking mothers. There was a couple saying a tearful goodbye, trying to embrace discreetly and kiss in public.

The air of sadness and uncertainty that was bearing down on the station platform overcame Valérie. The sight of the children still being evacuated touched her... she sent a silent plea to God to keep them safe. And if you could see your way to ending this infernal war, I'm sure we'd all be incredibly grateful to you... she hoped with all her being that someone somewhere heard her silently delivered prayer for them.

"Are you ok, Miss?" enquired a soldier standing to her right, his kit bag at his highly polished booted feet. He was only 18 years old, some mother's beloved son, brother, cousin.

"Yes, thank you, I'm fine. It is so sad... watching all these people still being moved around by the war. When will it end?"

"I wish I knew Miss, and then I might not have to go away."

"Do you know where you're being posted to? Oh! careless talk costs lives and all that."

"No, I don't know until I get there, Miss. You look like you're doing your bit too... typing for top brass? Making tea for pilots? Eh?"

His casually dismissive remark affronted Valérie. As if women's war effort jobs weren't quite at the same level of importance and contribution to the overall cause somehow.

"Actually, no... I listen to the incoming messages from France and decode them for the top brass as you call them... as important as making tea, I think." She knew she shouldn't have told him, but his flippant comments had bristled her.

"I didn't mean to... I'm sorry, Miss... I never meant that what you do wasn't important. I'm sorry."

Valérie saw that the young soldier blushed, suitably chastised. He had probably never seen many of his female relatives outside of their domestic roles in their homes until recently. Now they were working in men's jobs, making weapons, ammunition and all the paraphernalia of war in factories up and down the country. Women were taking a new, active and hardworking role in society. He looked so young, too young to be a man yet, but not a child either.

Valérie felt angry for the injustice that his generation had experienced war so soon after the Great War of 1914-18. The war to end all wars, the papers had called it. And yet here they were, at war again within three decades. The country still faced an uncertain future. Hitler's troops were only just over 20 miles away from the south coast, across the Channel in France. And she knew the enemy occupied the islands of Jersey and Guernsey, although not widely reported in the wireless news or the newspapers. This young soldier had his life in front of him. Well, she hoped and prayed that he did.

"Don't worry about it," she said to him.

The train came into view. The clouds of steam hissed and the smell of coal smoke swirled around and obscured their view of the locomotive as it stopped at the platform.

"Are you going to London?" he enquired, still a little embarrassed about his earlier remark and obviously trying to recover his standing in her eyes.

"Yes... they have asked me to go for an interview for another section... at least I think they have... it's all happened quickly. And I probably shouldn't have told you that either," she laughed.

She had observed a couple of such publicly inappropriate conversations over recent weeks–one in Smiths, the corner shop, between her two neighbours who were speculating on what the influx of American troops up at the airfield was all about. And then another conversation she had overheard between no less than three colleagues in the ladies' room, again being imaginative about the disappearance of another colleague, supposedly drafted into a division for special work.

"Don't you worry Miss, I promise your secret's safe with me, I'll take it with me to wherever I end up," he beamed back at her and gave her a cheeky wink.

"And I hope you bring it back safely with you," Valérie said as she glanced at her train ticket.

"I'll sit with you for the journey if you like Miss," the young man offered.

"I'm afraid that probably won't be possible... they have given me a first-class ticket, I'm not sure whether that's a mistake though... I've only ever travelled third class before... I'm sorry." She wasn't sure why she was apologising.

"Well, you make the most of it Miss, someone must think that you're important enough to go to London up front." The young soldier visibly grew in stature as he almost stood to attention.

"Thank you for your company, please travel safely wherever you are going to, and remember to write home to your family," ordered Valérie.

The young soldier stood to attention this time and saluted her.

"Yes, Miss."

10

Marianne

A week later

How many times during that week did I dial the number on the florist's card from the flower arrangement of the French stranger? And how many times did I not press the telephone symbol to make the call? And how many emails of thanks to friends and family did I compose, both long and short, and then deleted them? To say I was in a quandary was an inaccuracy. To say I was in a state of delicate suspension, finely balanced between a place of safety in the already known memories about mum, and the unknown 'things', that the photograph suggested, now that would be true. And heaped on top of this, I was missing grandma dreadfully and the routine of spending the weekends with her.

Four, or was it five days later? However many it was, I had to take some positive action and shake myself from this grieving stupor. I called my cousin David.

"David, hello, it's Marianne... yes I'm fine thanks... well, no - actually I'm not, I really miss grandma and I'm struggling to get motivated to do much. She took up all my spare time, not that I'm complaining, because I'm not – but when something suddenly ends, without warning it leaves an enormous gap in your life."

"Marianne, come on, that's not like you. They say time is a healer and you'll get over it... it takes time, that's all... if you want some company I can come over at the weekend. Or you could come over and see Aunt Ethel, she'd love to see you."

"I'm not that desperate for company, David! I'd rather wallow in my self-pity than deal with her professional state of mourning that she's perfected over the years."

David laughed. We both knew that Aunt Ethel was only happy when she had something or someone to moan about. As she'd got older, she'd become the eternal pessimist.

"Anyway, the reason I'm ringing you is that I wondered whether you could remember Aunt Ethel or Aunty Jean talk about anyone called Jacques being associated with the family?"

"No, never heard of him - why? Who was he?"

"I don't know... did you see the smart old man who turned up at the funeral last week?" Was it only last week?

"Yes, now you say that he asked me whether I was your brother. I told him I wasn't, and he asked me to point you out, but I couldn't see you anywhere... who was he?"

"I don't know David, it's a bit of a mystery, he said he knew my mum, he was in the war with her... but no one ever mentioned this name when I was a girl... it is odd isn't it?"

"Sorry Marianne but I have to go, another call on the line, sorry - I'll come over at the weekend alright?"

"Don't worry if you're busy, David, I'll be ok, Janet's next door... I'm lost without her to be honest."

So, I was no further forward finding out who this Jacques person was. I returned to the haven of the sofa.

Janet worried about me and it wasn't fair to give her the unnecessary burden to carry; she was a genuinely caring friend. She watched and noticed that I couldn't really settle to anything long enough to concentrate on it. Quietly and patiently she followed me and finished the tasks I had begun but left incomplete. She had also taken to cooking an extra portion and leaving it on the kitchen counter for me. My appetite had disappeared, but her tasty home cooking nourished and comforted me in my grief. It reminded me so much of grandma.

I recognised I had felt these feelings of sorrow before as a child when mum died, and so all of this had a somewhat unusually comforting familiarity about it. I remembered the empty feeling, a sense of hollowness, as though my heart was a void of nothingness. People say that you feel an immense hole within you. It was as true now as it was then. I reflected how if a child loses a parent now, there are mechanisms within schools and charities to work alongside them. Children are more supported in their grief. In 1943 there were no such things, only my beloved grandma. She allowed me to be angry and sad about something I didn't understand. How was I supposed to comprehend what it meant to a child's life that her mother wasn't coming back to our home? Grandma had held me in her arms and stroked my hair as I cried for something that I couldn't quite identify, but I knew I'd lost. It did not cross my mind then that she felt the same numbness as I did, and she was hiding it from me.

The more I dwelt on these things of the past, the more I had a sense, a deep intuitive knowing that grandma had been trying to tell me something when she insisted I take the old biscuit tin on the day of her birthday party. But what was it she hadn't said to me? And why hadn't I remembered to ask her about the photograph the day after I saw it for the first time. My annoyance and frustration with myself gnawed away at me.

The afternoon had passed unseen. It was dark when I shook myself out of the huddle I'd made under a blue woollen check patterned blanket on the oversize mushroom coloured sofa. I went to the kitchen to fetch the tin. With the blanket repositioned around my shoulders like a cape of protection, I prized the lid from the tin and placed it on the glass coffee table. Grandma's treasure comprised trinkets purchased from places visited, keepsakes, and invitations to occasions. Many mementos of a life well lived. Date order arranged theatre and classical concert tickets, travel tickets, receipts, even menus. Then there were so many photographs of holidays, birth-days, my graduation at which she had been so proud and emotional, family members, friends. Everything and everyone that she had held dear. They were all neatly labelled on the reverse with the names of the participants, the date, and the location.

She'd tied together the photographs of mum with a soft pale green ribbon that I recognised from my childhood. It was my school hair ribbon, and grandma had kept it all these years. I cried, not so much for myself but for her. She had experienced the grief of losing her only child, her daughter. I felt wretched for her now, whispering out loud, "That's not the direction that the circle of your life should have taken Grandma." I had never really noticed it when I was growing up. She had tried to protect me from the depth of her own feelings, and yet I had felt them permeating our life. I had carried the respon-sibility of her happiness for many years. As I stroked the soft, worn ribbon, I felt close to her, and I allowed the tears to flow.

After a while I found a tissue in my dressing gown pocket: another day that I hadn't got around to getting dressed. Wiping my tears away from my cheeks, I spotted the corner of an envelope at the very bottom of the tin. Carefully removing everything else, I lifted out the ageing item. It was unlabelled on the front. Very unlike grandma not to put any details on things. It had lost its gummed surface over the years and was quite brittle along the V shaped edge of the closure. I gently lifted the opening to reveal a document inside. I removed and unfolded it, then flattened it out on the glass table next to the tin.

The typed telegram was a stark statement:

NORFOLK 28TH SEPTEMBER 1943.

DEEPLY REGRET TO INFORM THAT YOUR DAUGHTER WAAF OFFICER VALÉRIE LILIANE BOUCHARD IS MISSING IN ACTION, PRESUMED DEAD STOP DIED SERVING KING AND COUNTRY STOP LETTER FOLLOWS STOP

COMMANDER HJ HUGHES-CLARK RAF.

The grim, formal words hauled a frayed childhood memory from the back of my mind. The man in a blue uniform and my grandma's ashen face in the cold sitting room. Sammy, my rag doll that had lost one of its blue button eyes. The memories gushed over me in a torrent of forgotten recollections. The wave physically knocked me back against the sofa. It was the telegram confirmation that mum had died during the war. I had not seen the telegram since that day, nor had I ever read the actual wording of it.

11

Valérie

London interview

The train ground to a halt. Steam hissed, and blackish grey smoke swirled around the front carriages. The brakes finished their high-pitched screech as she stood up to leave the red upholstered carriage. A man in a pinstripe suit holding a bowler hat and a quality leather briefcase opened the carriage door for her and bid her "good day, Miss."

The train guard opened the door of the First-Class carriages and guided her down the two steps to the platform.

Valérie straightened her jacket, smoothed down her skirt and gazed around at the thronging noisy station. People on the move. She looked around for the young soldier she had chatted to before the journey, but the platform was a churning sea of war weary and anxious faces.

"The exit is at the top of this platform, Miss."

"Thank you. I was told that a car would collect me... I don't see how that could be possible... there's so many people here!"

"Ah, I see Miss. Follow the crowds to the exit and there is a taxi rank on the right. If a car is collecting you, it will wait there."

The last car in the taxi rank queue was a replica of the one that had collected her this morning. She walked towards it. The driver touched his peaked cap, then opened the rear passenger door for her. He took his position behind the wheel.

"I'm afraid I don't know what address I'm going to, I'm sorry."

"Now don't you worry about that, I do, and I'll get you there in one piece. We'll have to make a detour though, another bomb last night near Regent's Park. And some streets are still closed since the Blitz."

As Valérie sat back in the seat, she realised she was again in the company of a man who was a stranger and heading for an unknown destination for a meeting she knew nothing about. She reflected that until recently some would think her behaviour scandalous. Who would have believed such a thing could happen to a young woman with a young child at home? How times had changed so quickly for women.

After 25 minutes of weaving through the dusty and crumpled streets of London, the driver turned right into a street and slowed down. The car stopped outside number 64. He opened the heavy door of the Crossley car, gave her a nod and pointed toward a gleaming revolving door.

"Here you are, told you I'd get you where you needed to be, Miss. Good luck."

She entered the rotating heavy timber and glass-panelled door and pushed it forward. Valérie caught sight of her reflection in the highly polished brass finger plates as she entered a grand foyer. What on earth was she doing here? She was nervous as she approached the front reception desk. The area felt like a cavern with its high colonnaded ceiling. Her footsteps echoed on the marble floor. A dark-haired woman of her own age smiled at her as she approached the reception desk.

"Good afternoon, may I help you?"

"Err, yes... err, I'm not actually sure who I'm here to see, but I have an interview, I think."

Who was she meeting? She had no names nor the address of this grand building. Suddenly she was aware of her situation. No one knew where she was and who she was meeting. She had told Winnie that they had asked her to swap to day shift for today, and her impending night shift would begin the following day.

"Aah, yes. And what is your name my dear?"

The friendliness of the receptionist's voice soothed her nerves a little.

"Valérie Bouchard."

"Thank you... ahh yes, you're the only one on the list for today. I'll just let the Captain know that you've arrived. Please - take a seat over there, Mrs Bouchard."

"Actually, it's Miss Bouchard."

"Ah, I see."

Valérie sat in a sumptuous blue leather armchair, savouring its softness. She glanced around and tried to focus on her surroundings to distract her racing thoughts. Why was she ordered to come here? The building was far too plush to have originally been a military property. She was trying to decide whether it had been a hotel and now requisitioned by the Government for a different use when a gentleman's voice interrupted her thoughts.

"Hello again Valérie, welcome to Baker Street. I trust you had a comfortable journey. Now, let's go up to my office where we can chat in private, shall we?"

The voice belonged to the unnamed man at the bus stop the previous morning. So he was an officer, a captain. But she still did not know his name. He had not introduced himself.

"Yes, of course."

Valérie knew she'd stuttered as he'd caught her off guard in her thoughts. She followed him, hoping that he hadn't noticed her fumbling nervously to gather her beginning-to-go-threadbare coat and handbag together.

"Could you send up tea for two to my office please Hilary?"

Valérie noted that like yesterday the manner and tone of his request held authority and was an order, albeit a polite order, to the receptionist.

"Of course Sir."

The lift stopped at the fourth floor. Valérie followed the Captain to his office. They had taken the journey in silence. Her mind raced as she suspected that this building was housing some kind of Secret Service, one that the public were not aware of.

"Let me take your coat, sit down and make yourself comfortable."

There was a knock at the panelled door.

"Come in... aah, here's our tea, thank you Hilary, biscuits too I see." He grinned.

They poured cups of tea with some discussion of whether the milk should precede the tea or vice versa, and that very few people could now take sugar because of rationing.

"Right, let's get down to business, shall we? You're probably wondering what all this is about and why we've asked you here Valérie."

"Well, yes... I am rather Sir."

"First things first then, allow me to introduce myself – I am Captain Selwyn Jepson. I am the senior recruiting officer for this section. It is my responsibility to recruit women for work within our division. This is not without vehement opposition from some quarters, I might add. However, Mr Churchill has approved our work and so we carry on looking for suitable candidates. It's not as if we can put adverts out in the press for the type of people we need." Captain Jepson laughed. Valérie did not understand why.

He took a brown paper file from his desk drawer and laid it in front of him. Even though it was upside down, Valérie could clearly make out her name typed on a square of white paper and pinned to the top right hand corner. Stamped in red across the middle of the file were the words CONFIDENTIAL F SECTION. She had an uneasy feeling about what information was inside the file.

"Why can't you advertise, Sir?" Valérie took a second biscuit from the plate. Biscuits were a long forgotten treat at home.

"Because of the type of work we do, undercover if you like."

"Do you mean you appoint spies?" Valérie looked at him wide eyed.

"No, not quite... our colleagues are not spies per se and our work is not spying in the conventional sense."

"Forgive me if I am missing your point here, Sir, but what does this have to do with me? Why am I here?"

He picked up a fountain pen and opened the file. He scanned down the first sheet of paper and worked down the second with the end of the pen until he stopped, halfway down a typed list.

"You wouldn't know this, but I was at school with your divisional leader, Group Captain Wilson. He has reported to us that your command of French is superb and your translations are impressively accurate. Tell me how... where did you learn to speak the language so fluently? I can't imagine they taught it in the school you attended."

Valérie was fairly sure that he hadn't intended to come across as so arrogantly snobbish, recognising that it was the inborn trait of the upper classes in society. For the second time that day, she felt affronted by a man's perception of what she should – or perhaps - shouldn't be. She felt a spark of annoyance rise inside her. It worked its way up to her throat, and she sat a little taller in her seat. She reached for the white china teacup and sipped her tea, replacing the cup silently in the saucer.

"No Sir, as you say, I wasn't taught the language at my local school. My Father was French."

Captain Jepson looked at the list in the file again, "Ah yes, our sources confirmed that your school in Bishop Street did not teach that subject on their curriculum. I believe you were studious while in class... And did your father teach you French from an early age? "

"Yes – and no. He would speak to me in English and then translate it into French and have me repeat it, correcting me as I went along."

Valérie recalled how Winnie would tick Phillipe off and say that the poor child would get confused about the correct words for things, and what good would speaking two languages do her, anyway. Her father would wink at her and carry on.

"Your transcription into the written form is excellent, Valérie. Did your father teach you to write in French too?"

"Thank you. Yes, he taught me a little and then when I was about 10 or 11 my teacher gave me French comprehension exercises after school... on a Wednesday I think it was."

"And did you learn anything else from this teacher?"

What an odd question, thought Valérie: her instinct told her she was being quizzed here. "I'm not sure what you mean, Sir. Do you mean did she teach me any other languages?"

"No, not languages. Did she take you to any other classes?"

Valérie looked at him squarely and sensed that this wasn't just about her ability to read and write in another language.

"Well, she took me to the amateur dramatics group she was part of, if that's what you are referring to."

"And I believe you played parts in a couple of productions, Valérie. Tell me about that – did you enjoy it? What did it feel like? Pretending to be someone else." Again he used that way of questioning that was a statement.

Valérie recalled the fun and laughter of rehearsals, costume fittings, of getting her lines wrong, but most of all she remembered she could turn herself into a completely unique person, with a new name and personality. It was her time when she could escape from the girls at school calling her names for being clever, 'the teacher's pet,' 'the class swot.' She knew she was frowning at Captain Jepson as she relived the memories for a moment.

"I loved every minute, I loved the way I could be in disguise and be someone else and escape into another world for a while."

She noticed he was making notes in the list's margin, "Mmm... useful," he muttered.

"I have a feeling Sir that you already know what I'm telling you."

He did not reply but stood up abruptly, crossed to the window and removed a silver cigarette case from his jacket pocket. He did not offer Valérie one.

Captain Jepson had left the file open on his desk. Valérie craned her neck to read the papers in it. And although the words were upside down, Valérie could clearly make out the typed information about her – and her family. They already knew everything there was to know about her – whoever 'they' were... She could see details about her background, her family, her unmarried status. And she could read Marianne's name. Her annoyance grew into an inward sense of self preservation. How much did he know about Marianne's father? Had the Captain been in pilot's training college with him? She knew she had to be very precise about what she said. They would find any untruths out.

Behind her, Captain Jepson smiled to himself. He had watched the reflection of Valérie in the mirror next to the window move forward in her seat and surreptitiously attempt to read the information in the open file.

He returned to his desk and stubbed out the cigarette butt in a glass ashtray.

"The war is now in its fourth year. The Government are becoming increasingly concerned about how much longer we can hold out against the Germans, even though the Allied support has helped and we remain hopeful. We can see glimpses of the tide turning in our favour in Europe. However, none of us really know what Hitler and the Axis have in mind – and if he took us by surprise and invaded, we don't think we could repel the Nazis. Do you think that is a fair assessment, Valérie?"

Valérie nodded. "The papers and the wireless tell us we must keep up the war effort and all do our bit... and that's what people are doing, Sir."

"Come on, Valérie, let's be honest here, you know as much as I do about what is going on, if not more."

"If I may be frank here Sir – then I think that – perhaps - what Mr Churchill and the Cabinet hear and read are not the actual daily field reports, the words of the people out there... do they really know what danger the agents in France are in? Do the Ministers really know how short of arms and supplies they are? How can they keep Hitler at bay when they have nothing to fight with?" Valérie knew she had overstepped the mark – but he had invited her opinion, hadn't he?

"We're working alongside the French Resistance movement as best we can with what we can provide – and much of that is providing personnel to organise and coordinate the best use of those weapons, explosives and resources and so on." The Captain was defensive in his tone.

"Yes, I'm aware of that, Sir. I think they are the unknown heroes of the war – putting their lives at risk to keep Hitler from advancing any further through France and crossing the Channel."

Valérie couldn't help but see her father in her mind's eye – how horrified he had been by the occupation of his homeland and dismayed, as were many French people, that the Government had allowed the invasion with no kind of effective fight. He had called the fall of France a mighty crash, 'un crash puissant.'

"Indeed," he muttered as he continued to scribble notes in the file.

Valérie wondered if her forthright response would get her in to trouble. She could not afford to lose her job.

Captain Jepson leaned back in his chair and lit another cigarette, "But we now seem to have hit a bit of a problem... we have an urgent need for more people on the ground in France."

"I'm sure we do, Sir," replied Valérie.

"And this is the reason we can't advertise for candidates – we can't be obvious about it... We need people who are sympathetic to the French cause. We can hardly put that in a small ad in The Times, now can we? The people we are looking for must speak French. And speak it fluently, like a native."

Valérie nodded as the dawning of an understanding formed in her mind, "I see."

Her heart raced in her chest. His comments arranged themselves in some kind of order in her head. She realised she was being assessed for something more than listening and translating other agent's messages. She wasn't sure just what she was being assessed for.

"Valérie, I hope you do – we need fluent French speakers like you but we also need a certain type of person who can blend in too. We need people that can be invisible, live under the Germans' noses without them seeing."

Valérie stared at him and noticed that his glasses needed cleaning.

"In a few moments I will take you to meet my colleague... she would like to ask you a few questions too."

Captain Jepson's statement confirmed her suspicion that she, as a woman, was being interviewed, possibly being recruited into other war work. Work that was being kept secret from the public and other military services. She breathed deeply to calm her nerves.

"I have a question for you, Captain – what is this division? Is this a secret division? Certainly not one that I have heard of."

"My colleague will explain this to you."

He had ignored her question. His vetting of her was over.

"Come, Miss Atkins is expecting us." And with that, he headed for the door.

Valérie hastily collected her coat from the ornate coat stand and followed him. As they walked along corridors and down a service staircase, then up several other carpeted staircases, Valérie observed she had been correct in assuming that the building had been a hotel in a previous life before the war. She felt certain that the circuitous route was deliberate. Was it to be a test of her memory or a way to confuse her so that she could not recall the direction in which they approached room number 326?

Captain Jepson gently tapped on the door and entered.

"Aah, there you are, come in."

A female voice spoke from the other side of a single suspended lightbulb, the owners' face concealed in the smoky shadows of the darkness.

"Sit down, Valérie."

The woman's voice was stern, and the invitation was a command.

They had stripped the room bare of any decoration and furniture: bare floorboards and a plain wooden table with two equally plain seats, each side of the table. All lit by the single unshaded lightbulb. As her cigarette smoke cleared, the dust motes floated about under the dim light.

Valérie sat as Captain Jepson took her coat and handbag from her and disappeared into the murky gloom.

"Now, you are here Valérie because I believe that you have some skills that could be useful to us and to your country."

Valérie nodded, hoping that she hadn't agreed to something. Shifting in the hard wooden seat, she realised that this small woman behind the desk had probably been listening in to the Captain's questioning. She was trying to place the woman's accent – Eastern European? She was unsure: she also realised that the woman had not introduced herself.

"First let me tell you who I am and what we do here. I'm Squadron Officer Vera Atkins, of the Special Operations Executive F Section. SOE for short. Our secret work in France is under Prime Minister Churchill's authority. We very much believe that we will hasten the end of the war by carrying out this work."

Vera took a cigarette from its box and offered Valérie one. Senior Service brand, she noticed.

"Thank you, but I don't smoke. I have to spend my money on my family, I'm afraid."

Vera lit up with an ornate silver and gold lighter that glinted under the lightbulb.

"So what is it you think I might do Squadron Officer that will help to bring the end of the war sooner?"

Vera rose from her chair and approached the front of the table: Valérie saw her clearly for the first time. A neat, slim woman with reddish hair. She had delicate hands and held her gaze while she continued to smoke in a considered way, as though savouring every drag of nicotine. She noticed she was not wearing the regulation uniform skirt but a pair of men's trousers and a sheepskin flying jacket. There was something about her: an air of authority, an assuredness, yet Valérie recognised an element of emotional intelligence in this woman.

Vera smiled at her and extended her hand. Valérie shook it.

"Please call me Miss Atkins, now I shall be direct with you, Valérie: we would like you to consider a move to another post within our special operational division. We think you fit the bill, although it will be a hard decision for you."

"And just what would this role involve may I ask?"

"We're inviting you to join us in the SOE Valérie, to join our French Section, F Section we call it. Not very original really."

Vera's intense eyes were upon her. Suddenly she smiled again, as though she had decided something important. Her face softened as she did.

"Valérie, you have skills we are looking for and we can teach you the rest. However, as I've said, I appreciate that this will be difficult for you. You'll need to go away to train and once you're ready, you will go to France to assist our field agents and the Resistance."

"I don't think that this would be possible, Miss Atkins... I can't leave my daughter and my mother."

"Aah yes, I'm aware of your situation at home... your records say that you have a small daughter... Marianne, isn't it? I perfectly understand that this will be a hard decision for you to make."

The silence felt thick and intense. It weighed down the air of expectancy in the darkened room. It was heavy with a thousand implications of what this meant for her, for Winnie, and most of all for Marianne. If she were to accept the transfer to this important role, how would they manage without her? Was it fair to ask her mother to be responsible for her daughter in wartime? What kind of message would this give to Marianne? That she had abandoned her? The reality that this was a dangerous and possibly life-threatening posting disturbed Valérie to her core. A wave of nausea came over her and she took several deep breaths to calm herself.

"So, if I were to accept your invitation, just what would it involve? How long would I have to go away for training? What kind of training? If I may say so you're asking an awful lot of an unmarried mother... I'm the breadwinner in our small family... if something happens to me, what will happen to Marianne? How would my mother be able to support her? And..."

"Valérie, please stay calm - you do not have to decide today. I assure you that in a worst-case scenario, which you are right to consider, then there will be some provision for Marianne. You have my word, I will, personally, make sure of that. We understand yours is an unusual case... your little girl needs you, I know... but, and I hesitate to say this... your country also needs you, Valérie, perhaps more so. Please believe me when I say that there are few women who have your particular and somewhat rare skills. And your passion for France."

Valérie felt dizzy with the enormity of the responsibility as a fresh wave of nausea threatened to rise and engulf her. She closed her eyes.

"Captain Jepson, could you fetch Valérie a glass of water?"

She heard the door open. A minute later he handed her the drink.

Valérie sipped it gratefully as Vera smiled at her again.

"I'm sorry... this has all come as a shock to me... I hadn't noticed that anyone was watching me while I was on duty."

"Of course, this is a lot to take in."

Valérie returned a weak smile to Vera. There was something caring about this unconventional and direct woman. She felt like she could trust her and her words.

"Now, to answer your question about training–this usually takes a couple of months. But go home and take some time to think over our request. We do not require you to be on shift tomorrow, Marianne."

"But I can't miss another!" Valérie protested.

"Listen carefully to me Marianne - obviously, you will need to speak with your mother about leaving Marianne with her, but please do not mention any other details of our conversation. You say that you are being transferred to an RAF base on the south coast to work with some new equipment. Now, the Captain will take you to the foyer and he will arrange for a car to take you back to the station. We will be in touch in a couple of days, when you have had time to consider things."

Vera approached Valérie, shook her hand firmly and placed her other hand on top. An unusual and friendly gesture for an officer, thought Valérie. This signalled that the interview was over, yet she had so many questions that she still needed answers to.

12

Marianne

Investigations begin

It must have been half an hour later when, with a trembling hand and a heart racing so fast it felt like it would run out of my chest, I picked up the phone and called the number on the florist's card. On the sixth ring, I was about to end the call.

"Hello, Richardson's florists, how may I help you?"

"Err... hello... erm, I'm not sure if you can help me... but I'm trying to find out who sent some flowers to my grandmother's funeral... it was last week."

"Let's see what we can do–did they order the flowers through the funeral directors? Or directly from us?"

"I'm sorry, but I honestly don't know. I only have your card that was in the arrangement...."

"Ok, so what was the name of the deceased's funeral please?"

"It was my grandma," I rambled, "Erm, sorry her name was Winnie Bouchard."

"That name rings a bell, just let me get the diary and have a look for you."

I heard the phone clumsily put down, presumably on the florists counter, fading footsteps and muffled voices. A tin bell rang as someone entered the shop. After a couple of minutes, the footsteps returned, and the assistant picked the phone up again.

"Hello? Yes, I knew I recognised the name. We did flowers for her 100th birthday recently, didn't we? I'm so sorry to hear that she has passed away. Right - I have the diary in front of me, what was the name on the flower card please?"

"A man called Jacques, spelt the French way, but there's no surname. I was wondering whether he gave you any details of his address... I need to contact him to say thank you and... and to find out how he knew my grandma."

"Let's have a look."

I could picture her running her pen down the list of orders and names for the funeral flowers, not quite knowing what she was looking for.

"I can't see anyone with that name... but there is a J Allard. The order was for an expensive flat posy of white, blue and red flowers... would that be the one?"

"Yes, that was it... did he give you an address at all?" I had unconsciously crossed my fingers and held my breath.

"Ah, I remember this one now," said the woman, much to my relief, "A French gentleman, paid by credit card. He insisted on paying in francs rather than euros... there's no address in the book... but give me a minute and I'll see if we still have the credit card details for the bank."

Again her receding footsteps echoed in my ear, returning briskly a minute later.

"You're in luck, the banking sheet is still here, not gone off to the accountants yet... but it doesn't have an address for him, only Mr Jacques P Allard then Perpignan, France I'm afraid."

"Oh, what a shame." My disappointment felt heavy. I hadn't expected it to be easy to find out who the stranger was, but a helping hand would have been nice.

"Did he leave a telephone number with you by any chance?" I asked, hoping and praying that he had.

"Mmm, no he didn't I'm afraid," was the next disappointing reply.

"Thank you anyway, I really appreciate your help with this."

"You're welcome. Oh, one other thing. He was insistent on the card being written in neat handwriting. He asked if we could do calligraphy, of all things! We've never been asked for that before. Anyway, I got my daughter to do it, she's an art student."

"Yes, it caught my eye for that reason. She did a lovely job of it. Oh, and by the way, all the flowers were lovely, thank you."

"You're welcome, my dear, I hope you find him, good luck. Bye now."

The phone went silent, but the thoughts clashed loudly in my head. So the stranger was Jacques Allard. Why had he sent flowers? Why had he travelled from France for my grandma's funeral? How did he know my mother? And how could I find him? I now had even more questions than answers.

Janet knocked as she stepped in the back door with a dish covered in silver foil.

"Penny for 'em? I've made Spag bol for tea tonight, that ok? I thought we might eat together. I think you need the company, my friend."

She placed the dish on the bench next to the hob. Then she pulled a high stool out from under the counter. Splashes of coloured paint were streaked across her old grey sweatshirt and her crazy hair escaped from under a purple headband.

"Janet, what would I do without you? Thank you."

"How long have you been sitting there, Marianne? What have you done this afternoon?"

"Far too long is how long! Right, you've spurred me into action!"

I went to the hob and organised a pan with some boiling water for spaghetti to go with the delicious smelling bolognaise sauce.

"You'll never guess what I've found out? I made a call to the florists that made up the arrangement that the French man sent to the funeral... and the lady told me he is Jacques Allard and he lives in Perpignan in France. The problem I have now is that he didn't give a street address or a telephone number."

"Really? Wow, Marianne, that's a turn up. So what are you going to do now?"

"Y'know what? I'm going to be really cheeky and ask our forensics and fraud team at work to see if they could find one for me tomorrow... it's a long shot I know but they might come up with something, they have international directories."

"And if they find it? What are you going to do then? Will you speak to him? This is so exciting! I told you it was like something out of a book or a film. And you're great at the details of things, Marianne. I've always thought that you should have been a detective, what with your fraud work at the bank and so on." Janet's enthusiasm and optimism were always a tonic.

I stirred the stringy pasta in the pan: there was something about it that always reminded me of yarn in grandma's knitting bag. Janet set out two plates and cutlery as I placed our meal on the counter. At that moment, I was grateful for our easy and supportive friendship. Janet had kept me on track over the last couple of weeks.

When our plates were full of the rich brown and red sauce on top of the aneamic looking carbohydrate a plan formed in my mind. I felt as though I had awoken from my stupefied fog of grief and my brain was waiting for some instructions for actions. A new clarity revealed itself, and I felt as though I had the energy to take on a new project.

"If, and it's a big if when I think about it, Janet, if I can find this Jacques, I'll ask him where he worked with mum. And I hope he might explain the photograph as well."

After my first good night's sleep for several weeks, I sensed that I'd turned a corner and life–my life–had to carry on after grandma's death. As I showered, I could hear her 'tut tutting' me her disapproval at wallowing in self-pity for too long. Well, that had to stop. And it would stop today now that I had a plan.

I blow dried my hair and saw that I needed a hairdresser's appointment. Then I dressed in some proper clothes. I felt human today and connected to the world I lived in rather than being self-absorbed in thoughts of the past, of a world that had gone.

In the kitchen I made a pot of tea and a proper nourishing breakfast of fruit, muesli and yogurt. How had I not noticed that I hadn't been making the first meal of the day for myself? This was the first proper breakfast I'd eaten for weeks; how easy it is to lose your routine when you're upset, I thought. Even Aslan seemed to sense the change in me as he curled around my legs and purred softly.

After making the much needed hairdresser's appointment for the following morning, I dialled the number for my colleague Mike Walters in the forensics and tracing team in London.

"Mike Walters here," his friendly North eastern accent sang.

"Mike, it's Marianne Bouchard here, how are you?"

"Marianne, hello! I'm canny thanks. But I thought you were on bereavement leave. I'm sorry to hear of your grandmother's passing... please don't tell me the Madrid job has changed and the lawyers have had you working, I thought they had submitted the evidence."

"Don't panic Mike, it's all going according to plan as far as I know, I'm sure I would have been one of the first to hear if it wasn't! What I'm ringing you for is... well, I need an international search doing on an individual... and... well, erm... it's off the record, between us."

I felt guilty as I knew my request was involving a colleague in a search for personal reasons and not related to a case I was working on. But so long as I didn't tell him that then he wouldn't be complicit in breaking company rules, would he? Error of omission of information and all that.

"I need to trace a man, in France."

"I'm sure there's plenty of French women who want to do the same," he chuckled, "Reet - so what've you got for me to go on? Let me guess tall, dark, handsome, smokes Gauloises cigarettes."

Mike's jovial attitude to his life spilled over into his work, and I realised that I'd missed the banter and camaraderie of the close-knit team over the recent weeks.

"You know what I mean! I have a name and I know which town he's in, sorry that's all."

"Oh, that's just great Marianne," his sarcasm came as expected, "And please don't tell he has the most average person's name in France, I have other, more urgent tracing of criminals to do for your department."

"I know, I know. Just when you have a few minutes Mike, I'd really appreciate it, there's a drink in it for you when I see you."

"Well, in that case, what's his name?"

I told him and he double checked the spelling.

"An address would be really useful, but anything you can find on him, really."

"Ok, leave it with me pet, I'll see what we can find. Does this have a case number? I'm guessing not, so I'll just put you down as the requestor reference. You know I have to put something Marianne."

"Yes, I know, that's fine," I said, sounding more authoritative than I felt. If there are questions later, then I'd come clean and face the music. They would mark my personnel file with a breach of procedure, but did it matter now? I intended to leave by the end of the year, anyway.

"Rightio, I'll get back to you as soon as I can. Ulterior motive obviously, then I can claim my pint from you."

"Thank you Mike, and if you find something for him, I might even get you a packet of crisps to go with it."

The conversation with Mike cheered me up no end as I returned the telephone handset to its cradle. Standing in the hallway, I opened the rarely used dining room door. I noticed that there wasn't the weeks' worth of dust that I expected. Yet another thing I would have to thank Janet for. The sun streamed in through the window and gave the room a glow that warmed it and me. So, in the absence of an office white board I decided I would use the dining room table to set out the bits of information I had about Jacques.

Then I located a half used roll of decorators lining paper, cut two lengths off it and stuck them together lengthways and attached it to the pale blue wall. My plan was translating into action and it felt good to be occupying myself with a challenge. If I were going to find out who Jacques was, then I would treat it like a fraud investigation. Everyone leaves a trace of their life in places, official documents and records, in photographs, within people's memories, their reminiscences and etched on their hearts - in the very act of living itself. If I looked in enough places and dug deeply enough, I felt sure I would find what I was looking for. I'd done it before - followed the trail of clues in the traces of life, and it had led me to the fraudsters they had paid me to find.

But this time it was personal and possibly more important. I needed to follow a trail of clues to lead me to a person who could tell me something about my mum. The thought was exciting and terrifying in equal measure. What if I find out something I wished I hadn't? What if this man disturbs my hazy memory of her and I learn something I didn't want to know? And then another thought struck me: what if this Frenchman wasn't who he said he was?

I laid out the photograph of Saint Girons; the card taken from the funeral flower arrangement and the telegram grandma had received in 1943 on the table. And then with a marker pen retrieved from my briefcase, I wrote six questions across the top of the length of paper on the wall:

Why? Where? When? What? Who? How?

I noted anything I knew about Jacques and mum under each heading and stepped back from the lists. Usually once these areas have some information I could form a picture from the patterns but not today I couldn't - I had so little information to go on.

A couple of hours had passed when I heard Janet in the kitchen.

"I'm in the dining room," I shouted through the house.

"There you are and look at you! All spruced up and looking human again. And you've been busy. Oh Marianne, I'm so glad to see you more like your old self again." She leaned lopsidedly against the doorframe and took in the scene before her.

"And I'm glad to be more like my old self, I can tell you. Yes, a productive morning too, so all's well."

"It's a lovely day, I thought I'd take you out to lunch, Marianne. It'll do you good to get out and get some fresh air, I think. It looks like you're investigating a crime, like something off a TV programme. Tell me what you're up to."

"Thank you, Janet, but I'm going to decline your invitation. But I shall take you for lunch as a thank you for everything that you've done for me over the last few weeks, my friend. Let's leave the car, walk to the riverside, and then we could have a celebratory bottle of wine."

"What are we celebrating?"

"Life. And how precious it is."

13

Valérie

Returns from London

Winnie looked up as she heard the soft click of the back door closing. As she entered the warm kitchen, she saw her daughter looked more tired than usual. Her face was pale and drawn after her long shift.

"What are you still doing up, Maman? You need your rest, looking after Marianne all day... has she behaved herself?"

Winnie smiled at her, touched by the French endearment that Philippe had taught her as a child. She went to the back door to double check Valérie had pulled the blackout curtain tightly across the glass pane. It was a habit she felt that she'd perfected for a lifetime, not just four years. Back in the cosy kitchen she went to the stove and lit the gas under the kettle.

"You'd like a cup of tea?"

"I can get my supper... although I'm not hungry... I had a sandwich from the canteen at work." There was the first lie to her mother, thought Valérie. It was as easy as that. Just say the words convincingly. Winnie busied herself preparing the teapot and two cups.

"I'll save the bread for tomorrow then, if you're sure you don't want supper."

Valérie shook her head, "Let Marianne have it for her breakfast."

"How was your day then? I know! I'm not supposed to ask! But you didn't seem like yourself this morning as you left for the base Val... and that makes me worried... is everything alright? Has something happened?"

She glanced at Valérie and saw at once that there was something troubling her dark eyes. She loved those eyes; they reminded her so much of dear Phillipe.

"Not much gets past you, does it? And there was me thinking that I'd put on a good show."

Valérie removed her coat and shoes and placed them next to Marianne's smaller version in the cupboard under the stairs in the hallway.

Closing the kitchen door quietly so as not to waken her little girl, she went to Winnie and hugged her. Winnie felt the anxiousness in her daughter's body and heard her sigh.

"Oh Mum, it's been a day."

The kettle whistled softly. Winnie removed it from the stove with a tea towel wrapped around the handle. The steaming water splashed into the teapot.

"Come on now, sit down next to the fire, well what's left of it anyway... and tell me what's happened."

Valérie sat in her father's old chair next to the dying embers in the grate. She wriggled her feet in front of the fading heat and took the cup of tea from her mother. The warm liquid and the glow of the grate comforted her. She felt her body relax after the tough day, but her mind was still racing with what she had learned and what the officers had asked of her. She closed her eyes and a sigh, unintentional, escaped from her lips. Valérie knew she was about to lie again to her dear mother. But how far and how much could she hide the truth? What was she going to disguise it as? Should she mention the trip to London?

She opened her eyes and held on tightly to the cup with one hand, hoping that Winnie would not see her shaking hand. Her heartbeat was loud in her ears and it felt fluttery in her chest. Valérie noticed she had, unconsciously, crossed her left middle finger and forefinger behind her back. Something she had not done since childhood, the playful act that was a precaution against telling a lie, by asking God's forgiveness before breaking one of the Ten Commandments. She did not uncurl her fingers.

"Well... I didn't actually go on shift today... two people came from London to talk to some of us in the listening room. They mentioned how well I speak and translate French. They said my skills were excellent and really useful to the war effort... and that they could use me somewhere else."

Valérie tried to keep her voice even and neutral, knowing that her mind and her heart were screaming at her to just tell the truth. It would be easier. Surely she could tell her own mother. It wouldn't do anyone any harm, would it? She could swear her mother to secrecy by crossing her fingers in front of her for luck.

"So your father's French lessons paid off then! Where did they say they could use you?"

Valérie tried to avoid Winnie's gaze by diverting her attention.

"Is there anymore tea in the pot, Mum?" The diversion had worked as she held out her cup for a refill.

"There's no milk left though... so who were the people from London? It seems a long way to come to talk to you."

"That's what I thought, they said that there is some new equipment that they are using at another air base on the South coast... they'd like me to test it out and if it works better, then I will train others to use it... it's supposed to have a better reception of the radio signals, clearer and more accurate and be so much faster... the two men were divisional leaders I think... one was an older man and the younger one was rather good-looking if I'm honest."

For the second time that day she felt nauseous - the enormity of the lies and the ease with which she was telling them appalled her. She felt sickly and lightheaded.

Winnie grinned at her, "Now our Valérie, don't you be having your head turned by another good-looking pilot... you know what happened last time!... we have enough to cope with now."

Valérie smiled weakly at Winnie, relieved to feel that her voice and the yarn she was spinning her mother were plausible so far.

"The thing is Mum... this air base is right down on the South coast and I will have to stay there for a while. Well, it could be a few months."

"And did you tell these people that you have a young child? Do they expect you to just go gallivanting off, miles away with her? Where would you live and who would look after her Valérie? I don't much like the sound of this love. I have to say, I think it's selfish of them to ask you. And it certainly wouldn't be fair on Marianne... she wouldn't know anyone, she's just a child, she's already experienced enough in her young life."

Winnie's grey eyes were wide with a fierce, steely determination to protect her granddaughter. Valérie felt her mother's fear of the unknown radiating into their kitchen and sensed Winnies' usual need to know the practicalities of any situation. This potential threat to their little family would hurt her, she knew that. She had come this far with her deception. Could she go back and undo it now?

"Well, that's the thing Mum... I wouldn't be able to take Marianne with me... I would need you to..."

Once Valérie had spoken it out loud, the damn of emotion broke. The tears flowed down her cheeks.

"Oh, my love, of course you couldn't take her away from her home. She would have to stay here with me."

Valérie found her handkerchief, wiped her tired, gritty eyes and blew her nose loudly.

"Oh Mum, it's such a big thing to ask of you though... but I know I have to play my part and try to make things better for all of us... and I know Papa would have wanted this too... I hate to think what has happened to his family in France - my aunties and uncles and my lovely cousins."

Valérie blew her nose again. The thoughts of and feelings for her father who had died in the air raid in Shaw Street while he was on fire duty in January were still raw, "I have to do my bit for the war effort."

Winnie listened to Valérie's words, hearing the passion and conviction in her voice as she talked of this possible new posting.

Valérie glanced up and saw that Winnie sat in silence as her tears escaped and rolled down her cheeks.

"Phillipe... your father would have been so proud of you, Valérie. And don't you dare tell me not to worry – I'm not daft, I know that being on an airbase on the south coast isn't one of the safest places to be at the moment."

Winnie knew Valérie wanted to change the world, and it's future. The fighting couldn't go on forever, and she knew her daughter believed in a peaceful future for herself and Marianne. She also knew that her daughter was realistic enough to know that she couldn't do it alone. She knew in her heart that her father's untimely death had motivated Valérie into taking practical action by carrying through her decision to join the WAAF. But Winnie also felt the weight of the question and its responsibility being asked of her. Could she make her contribution and do the work she was being asked to do by caring for her granddaughter single handed? And how could she let her only daughter go? How would Marianne cope with her mother working away? What if something happens to her? The questions came in a barrage of thoughts into Winnie's mind.

"I'm sure I'll be fine, Mum: the clever people in the RAF, the scientists, and so on have developed some new machines that tell us that the German bombers are approaching the mainland before they get here. That would give us a better chance to get to the bunkers, but I'm sure my new job would be underground anyway, like it is now. Anyway, I haven't decided yet – they've given me a few days to think about it and talk to you about it."

She had easily set another half lie free into the room as it rolled off her tongue.

"Mmm... I know you have to go Valérie, for all of us, the war needs to end, and soon... and I'll look after Marianne the best I can with what we've got, and..."

"Don't Mum... I know you will."

"Valérie, you must do what you know is right... now, it's probably time we both tried to get some sleep."

14

Marianne

The search continues

After my newly cut and coloured hair appointment with my hairdresser Claire, I felt renewed and refreshed. A complete change of style and tone seemed appropriate as I headed into a new phase in my life. It felt good to be out and about, interacting with people after the blurred early days of grief.

Next I went to the second floor history section in the town library, not sure what I was looking for. Any reference to Saint Girons in the Second World War would be useful. I found a couple of books about France during the war, and there was half of a shelf of books on the French Resistance that I dismissed. There was little information other than locating the place on a map.

I took the book with the map in it to the Librarian's desk.

"Excuse me, may I photocopy this page from this book, please?"

"Hello, yes, of course. It's 10p per copy, is that ok?"

I nodded, "Could you make that three copies then please? I'll push the boat out."

The Librarian grinned, "Page 49?" she checked as I handed it over to her.

She passed the copies and the book back to me in exchange for thirty pence.

"Actually, could you tell me where I can find some information about a town on the map you've just copied. I'm trying to find out about a small place called Saint Girons in southern France, during the War and also about the WAAF... do you know where I could look please?"

"Erm, let me see—I suppose it depends on what significance the town had during the war, really. Was it the place of a battle do you know?"

"I don't know, I'm sorry," I replied.

"I don't think you'll find very much about wartime France in our library here—lots of locals collect and publish the parish history, but global history... we hold little of that, I'm afraid. It's a long shot, but if British troops had a connection to your French town, then you might find something in The National Archives at Kew. Oh, and you could try the War Museum in London."

"Do you think so? It's worth a look, I suppose. Thank you for your help."

Two days later, as I scanned my information display on the dining room wall, the phone rang in the hallway. It was the relentlessly chirpy Mike Walters.

"Marianne pet, I think I've found something for your Frenchman - do you want the good news or the bad news first?"

"The good first, please Mike."

"Well, I've found an address for you. Write this down, it's 18 Rue des Acacias, Clara-Villerach, it's near a place called Prades, west of Perpignan when I looked it up. Near the Spanish border and the Catalan region. It looks like it's in some foothills."

"Thanks Mike, that's wonderful. And the bad news is?"

"No telephone number, I'm afraid."

"Oh well, you can't win them all, but that's great thank you. Anything else on him?" I held my breath. Please let there be something else on him, please, I silently begged.

"No, not really, nowt criminal anyway. He's not wanted by Interpol or anything like that. Financial records show he appears to be comfortably off, I'll post out copies of the bits and pieces I found on him. Oh, one thing I found that was interesting was that they gave him the Order of Libération, a French honour for outstanding service during the war."

"Mmm, that is interesting... I wonder what he did that deserved a medal? Yes, if you could just post the things to me Mike rather than record anything internally I'd be grateful, thank you. Pay for the postage and I'll refund the cost when I see you."

Again, I felt guilty that Mike was taking a risk for me without knowing why. The need to exchange some information with him was strong, but I knew that was to ease my conscience more so than his. I also knew Mike of old, we'd worked some long hours together for over 10 years on some tough jobs. I knew it would intrigue him to know why I need to find out who Jacques Allard was.

"So, c'mon Marianne, spill the beans - who's this Jacques gadgie?"

I laughed as he slipped into his Geordie dialect.

"I'll be honest, Mike and don't laugh but I'm not really sure... he might've been a friend of my mum's, from the war. But as far as I know, the WAAF stationed her on the south coast at an RAF base that was bombed. He turned up at my grandmas funeral, it was very odd."

"Oh blimey, it sounds like an international mystery pet, good luck with that."

"Thanks again, Mike."

"You're welcome, you've only got to ask if you need me to look for anything else for you." Mike was a genuine bloke and had always been happy to be a bit of a maverick if need be. I knew he meant what he said.

Ten minutes later, with a cup of tea in one hand and the marker pen in the other, I surveyed the information chart again after adding these additional details. No, I still couldn't see a pattern emerging. They were just unconnected words before my eyes. Names, places, and some dates, but there was nothing that linked them together. Feeling frustrated, I questioned myself: surely I hadn't lost my investigative touch so quickly?

Well, at least I had an address: I would write to Jacques and see what happens. He might not reply, he hadn't really introduced himself at the funeral. It was as though he'd briefly stepped out of the shadow of the past and then wished to disappear again back into it.

I set to composing a letter to send to Jacques Allard and after four attempts the tone sounded about right. Thanking him for his time to attend grandma's funeral and the gorgeous flower arrangement with the poignant message, I hoped it sounded both friendly and politely inquisitive. Next I enquired how he had known Winnie and my mother in particular.

"It sounds perfect to me. Let's see what he responds with. I know I keep saying it, it's very exciting, Marianne. Who knows where it might lead you." If Janet approved of the wording in the letter, that was good enough for me.

"Mmm, it's a bit nerve-wracking if I'm honest... what if I find out something that I wished I hadn't?"

Somehow we seemed to have settled into a routine of a having a take-away on a Thursday evening. As I disposed of the empty cartons and wrappings, I wondered yet again how mum and Jacques had met.

"I know mum had been to France before the war, before she had me, to visit grandpa's family. Perhaps she'd met Jacques then? I wonder whether he was a friend of my grandpa or his family?"

"It's a workable theory, I suppose. I can post the letter for you tomorrow if you like. I need to go into town for some shopping, anyway. Do you want it sending by Air Mail?"

"If you don't mind, that would be great, thanks Janet."

I sat down, sealed the envelope and handed it over the kitchen counter to her.

"We need a toast to send your greetings on their way to France, cheers," said Janet as she raised her glass of white wine and I did likewise.

"Cheers. Here's to its safe arrival."

"So, what are you going to do while you wait for a reply? Are you going back to work next week or did you speak to your Director about taking some time off?"

"No, actually I'm not going back for another three months... I spoke to him yesterday and we've agreed I'll be taking a sabbatical until the end of August. I told him I have family business to sort out and that I need to travel to do it. He was fine about it, he even suggested that it be the start of my wind down to leaving in November. That suits me perfectly, to be honest. And the solicitor tells me that grandma had rather more savings than I was aware of."

"Oh Marianne, that's wonderful news about work time off and Winnie's savings! She always struck me as a woman who watched the pennies."

"Yes, she was. When I was little, I can remember that she could make a meal out next to nothing... after the war she used to make a pie out of a potato, an onion and a tin of stewed steak and put a pastry crust on the top of it. I think it was the tastiest thing I ever had." In my reminiscence of it I could taste her pastry.

"Anyway, I'm thinking that as I'll have the time and the funds, I'm going to visit my cousins in France. You never know, I might even get to meet Jacques while I'm there. I'd love to hear what he did in the war to get an award afterwards."

Janet nodded in eager approval: I could tell she was thinking some-thing through. Her eyes sparkled when she did.

"What do you think about this for an idea? Do you want a sidekick on your travels? Every good detective has a partner that makes them look good... I could do the stuff like, erm, book the hotels and make the travel arrangements while you do the investigating and finding out about Jacques? And if I'm a rubbish sidekick, you could sack me and I'll just be a faithful travelling companion instead. I could do with a holiday, anyway."

Taken aback at her offer, I quickly saw the benefits to both of us. And we enjoyed one another's company.

"Really? Would you come with me, Janet? We'd have some fun, even if the whole thing of tracking down Jacques doesn't lead to anything. You'll like my French relatives and I haven't seen them for nearly two years. Time passes so quickly."

"I'd love to go with you, we'll have a road trip like *Thelma and Louise*."

"God, I hope not Janet! Susan Sarandon drove them off the edge of a cliff!"

"Oh, did they? That's not the film I'm thinking of, is it?" Janet frowned and then laughed.

"Seriously though, I'd love the company and I'll help you with the travel costs. Grandma would be happy about that; she'd have thought that spending some of her money on a friend was fitting."

"No, I'll pay my way Marianne."

"Look, I will not argue with you. She would have wanted me to help someone else with some of it, I'm sure."

"Ok, but I'll only accept if you let me treat you and your cousins to a dinner one evening."

"Right, that's a deal," I said as I held out my hand and we shook on it.

"When are you thinking of going?"

"Well, I'll need to ring Alain, Simone and Marie-Clare, my cousins, and see when they're free for us to visit. And then I suppose it'll be a matter of waiting for a reply from Jacques. If he will meet me, then he's not so far from the Ariege area where the cousins are. I'll make some phone calls to them tomorrow."

15

Valérie

Decisions

"So, are you feeling better now Valérie?" Celia's question as she came out of the toilet cubicle behind her made her jump and return to the present.

"Yes, I am… thanks."

Celia retrieved her comb from her bag, ran it through her blond curls and smoothed her uniform down, appraising herself in the mirror over the sink in the cramped ladies' restroom. She had always had that air of confidence and knowing that people looked at her, that she turned heads, thought Valérie.

"There you are. Your turn now." Celia stepped aside from the mirror. She offered Valérie her comb as she allowed her to take her place in front of it.

Valérie stared at herself in the pitted glass. She looked tired. The two previous sleepless nights were taking their toll. She was grateful to whoever had changed her scheduled night shifts into days this week. Was it Captain Jepson or Vera Atkins that had intervened? She suspected it was one of them. The last few days had been hard going. Juggling the tasks of listen intently while on shift, with the thoughts and anxiousness in her head about the decision she needed to make. The urgency of indecision was growing louder. Valérie knew they would expect a decision from her any day. And she worried about how Captain Jepson or Vera would contact her. They had not actually said how they would do so. She hoped they wouldn't come to her home. How would she explain that to Winnie without revealing that she had lied to her?

The reflection staring back at her appeared to be more determined than she felt. She smiled at herself and straightened her shirt as she tucked it into her skirt waistband that was now too big for her. She had observed how all the girls in her listening and translating group had lost weight over the last few months, as the ration coupons bought less and less.

"So, tell all Valérie... who was the man you were talking to at the bus stop the other morning? No one has seen him around the base before... he looked like an officer... someone you know and haven't told me about, eh?" Celia winked at her.

Valérie laughed at Celia's implied suggestion and then realised that she was going to have to lie, yet again, and to her oldest friend. She couldn't see another way out of this awkward question. This telling of untruths was becoming a habit.

"Yes, he is a Captain... and no Celia Jenkins, it's not what you think either. He'd been for a walk away from the base... and err, got lost... and we got chatting." Valérie thought this story sounded lame, even to her. Would Celia be convinced?

"You must have had plenty to talk about. The girls noticed you didn't turn up on shift... and Mills wasn't happy when you weren't there, she had to put the headset on herself and cover for you," she grinned.

"That's right, I didn't feel very well, and the gentleman walked me back home. And no, before you ask, he didn't ask to see me again. And he's not an American."

Valérie knew she would have to cut this conversation short with Celia or else risk tripping herself up with the fragile web of lies that she was constructing. Plus, Celia had a habit of often being the source of gossip on the base.

"We'd best get back, Old Millsy will have our guts for garters if we're late back from our lunch break."

An hour later, Valérie looked up to see Section Officer Ruth Mills enter the room with their Group Captain. Usually they were told of Group Captain Wilson's visits to the operations and listening sections. Valérie knew Mills was approaching her desk and once she had her attention, she beckoned her with her forefinger to follow her.

So this was how they were contacting her. She stood to attention and made her way towards the bomb proof door as requested, noting Celia's raised eyebrows as she passed her desk.

Out in the corridor, he shook her hand, "Ah, Miss Bouchard, it's good to see you again. Thank you Miss Mills, I need to have a word with Miss Bouchard in private, please."

Valérie noted her Section Officers' surprised look at being dismissed. She'd obviously expected inclusion in any conversations with the Group Captain. The traditional hierarchy of the RAF officers' ladder had merely transferred itself into the WAAF. Valérie's heart sank as she recognised that she would have to construct another strand of lies to add to her growing web of deceit. Mills, Celia, and the others would ask her what her removal from duties was about. She would have some more false explaining to do.

"Come, let's get some fresh air away from this rabbit warren down here."

He courteously opened the door to the staircase leading above ground. Once outside, he breathed deeply, filling his lungs with the fresh air.

"I know how you feel Sir, I do exactly the same when I finish my shift."

"I'm not surprised, I don't know how you girls do it, working underground like that, you're like moles."

He offered her a cigarette. She declined.

"Now Valérie, may I call you Valérie?"

"Yes, of course, it is my name, Sir."

"It seems a little too formal to address you as Miss Bouchard, especially as we need to discuss something of a somewhat personal nature... I expect you've already deduced that I am here at Jepson's and Vera Atkins' request."

"Could we walk as we talk, Sir? I don't want to draw any more attention to myself."

Captain Wilson grinned at her again. He had noticed her ability to blend into any situation on previous occasions. Despite his initial reservations about knowing Valérie had a small daughter, he now felt justified in passing her name forward to his old pal and colleague Jepson.

"Of course... I've been hearing excellent reports from Jepson and Miss Atkins, you impressed them when they met you last week."

"Thank you, Sir... it all happened quickly and their request came as a shock... I presume you know what they have asked of me?"

"Yes, I'm aware... or shall we say, I'm aware of their type of work."

They walked a little further, past an open aircraft hangar. The noise of the engineers repairing damaged aircraft and the smell of aircraft fuel mingled together.

"And have you reached a decision, Valérie?"

Her heart stopped for a moment. This was the moment of truth. Had she decided? They walked in silence a while longer. Could she play for a little more time to decide? The calm and rational decision process in her head over the last few days had left her exhausted. It had moved into her night times and her heart as she grappled with the merits of the right course of action to take. Valérie took a deep breath.

"The thought of leaving my daughter and my mother, then putting myself in a life-threatening situation in a foreign country makes no common sense at all. And yet when I think about it half an hour later I know it is my duty – to Marianne, to my mother and especially to my father's memory. I suppose it's an honour that they have asked me to do my duty for my country."

Her heart and her mind had travelled back and forth between the opposing ends of the same spectrum for three days now. The Captain nodded.

"I think I nearly have Sir... do you think Miss Atkins would let me have until tomorrow to decide for definite? I'm sure you understand Sir – this isn't something I can decide easily... not where it concerns Marianne."

"I'm sure she will allow that Valérie, let me place a telephone call to her when I return to my office."

"Thank you Sir, I would appreciate that."

16

Valérie

Leaving Marianne

That evening, although invited, again sleep did not arrive. Valérie lay awake, feeling nervous about what was ahead. She was cosy and warm in her bed with her sleeping daughter, her little Marianne held close to her. She hoped that there would not be any air raids this evening to interrupt their rest. Softly stroking the girl's hair, she prayed she was doing the right thing in leaving this happy-go-lucky little one in her mother's care. She knew with a certainty that burned within her she could not stand by and watch others make great sacrifices and not do her bit for the war effort. And they had offered her the opportunity to use her ability to speak fluent French to help bring the end of the war closer.

Yet again she recalled the interview with the officers in London when they asked her if she would undertake some special operations for her country. She smiled to herself at the memory of asking, "So do you think that I'm a suitable candidate, Sir? I'm not sure what skills I have that can help you... and we're already short of listeners and translators in my division." How naïve she had been. 'They' had someone who had been watching her for what? Weeks? Months? Someone that she had been unaware of had been observing, then reporting back about her. But who was it? Valérie supposed it didn't matter now.

In the still darkness she found the conviction within her decision melted as she listened to her daughters' soft, even breathing. The sleep of the innocent. How could she leave her? Was she abandoning her to a life of being an orphan if she did not return from her work in France? She had guessed that this work would aid the Resistants to the Nazi regime that still occupied the country and she knew she would go to a dangerous situation; she'd have to think on her feet every day to stay safe. And to stay alive.

Her thoughts panicked her as they bombarded her imagination. What if the Germans captured her? Or they shot or hanged her? What if she ended up in a work camp with other enemies of the Third Reich? Just what provision would the War Office make for Marianne and Winnie? She had made a simple will, just in case... not that she had anything of any value to leave to them. But she had her life, she was Marianne's mother, Winnie's only daughter. Surely that was precious, and she owed them that?

With too many thoughts swirling in her mind; sleep was avoiding her. The feeling of her heart aching lay still and heavy in her chest. Yet it was moving and growing into something far bigger. Her slumber starved thoughts and worries were evolving into one identifiable and overriding mass: guilt. She felt guilty for what she was about to put her dear family through. It was pinning her to the bed in the depths of the early hours. What if she declined their offer on the telephone tomorrow? All of this would just go away.

But what if she didn't go? What if she didn't make her contribution and sacrifice like so many other men and women were? She shifted slightly to release her numb arm from beneath Marianne's neck, pulled the covers over her and closed her eyes. In the silence of her childhood bedroom she was sure that she heard her father's voice whisper, "You must go my cherie Valérie... France needs help. I am so proud of you... and one day Marianne and the daughters of this generation will be as well."

She opened her eyes, but there was no one there. A calmness seeped through her as she closed them again, noticing the aching feeling in her chest had gone. Valérie slipped into a deep sleep. The comfort of a right decision cocooned her after all.

17

Marianne

Decisions made

I spent most of the following morning in long conversations with my French cousins Marie-Clare, Alain and Simone arranging dates for the following month to visit them. It had been far too long since I had last spoken to them at length and caught up with their lives and news. The last brief calls I'd made to them was to tell them that their father's sister-in-law, my beloved grandma, had died. Unfortunately, none of them could travel to England for her funeral. This made the appearance of the French stranger even more remarkable. Time passing had surreptitiously struck again: the blink of an eye can steal two years from your life.

Next I stood, yet again, in front of my information chart in the dining room, trying to see the gaps, the connections and what I needed to ask Jacques. There were too many holes and as I scanned the things I knew, my thoughts switched to an additional question. What was it I didn't know about my mother? I took two sheets of paper, wrote Valérie across the top of the first and Jacques on the second. I jotted some questions and notes down on both sheets and placed them alongside the photographs and other paperwork I had gathered together on the dining table. What was I missing? Something didn't add up somewhere, but I couldn't put my finger on it. There was a missing link in the information. Surely something there must be a clue?

After a sandwich lunch, I picked up the phone again and dialled the next number on my to do list.

"Hello, Imperial War Museum, how may we help you?"

"Yes, hello, could I check your opening times please?"

"Yes, we're open 10am until 6pm Wednesday to Saturday. Wednesday is our quiet day, and it's best to book for specific exhibitions," said the efficient voice.

"Thank you. I'm just looking for information about my mum during the war. She was in the WAAF. Do you have any of their archives there?"

"Yes, we have some, it depends on what you're looking for, really."

I laughed, "The thing is I'm not sure what I'm looking for, it'll be a case of I know it when I see it I think."

"One of our staff will help you locate records if we hold any on the subject you're looking for, but I'm sure you'll find the museum interesting, anyway."

"Thank you, I'll ask someone to help me. What is the nearest tube station please?"

"You've got a choice, depending which direction you're travelling from. Either Lambeth North or Elephant and Castle, and we're a short walk from either."

"Thank you, that's really helpful. Bye for now."

Finally, I dialled the last number on my to do list, listened to the unanswered rings and then pressed re-dial. As I looked at the wall chart again, it drew me to the column labelled When? The dates I'd written in were all in 1943, the year mum died.

"Good afternoon, National Archives Kew, which department can I connect you to?"

The pleasant voice cut across my concentration on the information on my wall.

"Hello, yes, erm, could you tell me whether you hold any information on the WAAF during 1943? I'm trying to find out information about my mum who served in it."

"Yes, I think we would hold records on that. Would you like to book some time in our reading rooms? One of the staff will point you in the right direction of specific records." The pleasant voice came across as relentlessly helpful, too.

"If that's possible yes, could I book for Friday morning please?" I didn't know what I was going to look for, but I had a deep feeling that by looking at original records I might find my clue to the missing links in what I already had.

Later that afternoon, I heard Janet close the back door and speak to Aslan.

"I thought I'd find you in the operations centre here. Any progress with your investigations today?"

"Yes, and no. Nothing concrete in terms of Jacques. You posted my letter, didn't you? How much do I owe you?"

"Yes, the man at the counter said it should get there on Friday. And don't worry about the cost, you can treat me to a coffee sometime."

"Thanks, Janet. Now how are you fixed for a French road trip in four weeks' time? The weather should be lovely in June and I'll even allow you to pack that ridiculous sun hat that you wear," I teased her.

"You spoke to your cousins? Oh, the timing is perfect for me, I'll have the painting commission finished by then. I'm really excited about this Marianne. Thank you for asking me to go with you."

"I think you invited yourself along, Janet!"

"Oh, I did, didn't I?" She laughed.

"My cousins are free to see us then, and the best bit is that they all insist we stay with them so it'll save on hotels. So, I thought we could do that first and then, when I hear from Jacques, I'll write again to him and see if we can visit him after the cousins. Does that sound ok to you?"

"It sounds great, Marianne."

"Talking of Friday, are you doing anything? Fancy a trip up to London on the train with me?"

"Yes, sure. Where are you going?"

"To look in the archives at Kew and the War Museum and see what I can find out about what women in the WAAF did - and whether there was a branch or a division or something of them in France. After all, mum was the daughter of a Frenchman. But if it sounds too dull a way to spend the day, you can change your mind, I'm not offended."

"No, I've never been to either, we can make a day of it."

"Right, that's sorted then."

Yet another sleepless night as I tried, without success, to access any deeply hidden memories of my missing mother. I searched amongst the remnants of images in my mind in the long hours of the early morning for something, anything that might give me the whisper of a clue. I was looking in my past for a recollection, a shadow of something from my childhood that told me something about who Lucille and Claude were.

18

Marianne

Childhood memories

As I tossed and turned, I relived my earliest memory of her. It was a painful one, but only in the sense that I was physically hurt. In the sleepless night, the picture of the event in my mind was a snapshot, a moment frozen in time. It was one of love and security, all wrapped up with softness and caring.

As I lay in the dark, I remembered we walked to the park hand in hand. Mum carried our gas masks. Her amusement at what she called my 'incessant chattering about everything that comes into your head' was a sweet sound. To my young ears it was a pure, tinkling and wispy kind of laugh that sounded like fairies dancing around her. Her laughter made her nose turn up at the end and crept up her face into the dark pools of her eyes. On that warm early summer 1943 day, the sunlight in her eyes made them shimmer between a dark brown black to a deep ocean blue as they reflected the cloudless sky in them.

We sat on a blanket on the grass with a picnic: a shared sandwich and for me, a rarely seen apple, sliced into the thinnest of slivers. "It will make it go further," grandma had said. Heaven knows where she had got it from or how many ration coupons she had saved, bought or swapped. It was a shiny red skinned apple. Of course my rag doll

Sammy had come along too, the much played with and slightly grubby doll that my grandpa Phillipe had given me last Christmas before he died. And of course she shared in the picnic, as rag dolls do.

As we sat in the sunshine, she picked daisies out of the grass and strung them together. The delicate little incision she made into each stalk with her fingernail mesmerised me. The gentleness of the perfectly executed exercise still moves me to tears even now. She placed a string of tiny yellow and white flowers carefully over my head. The necklace hung around my neck. Then patiently she began the same process again. This time she placed a smaller version of the necklace on my head.

"I crown you Princess Marianne and may you always have good luck and love on your side," she stated solemnly.

"I don't want to be a princess Mummy, I just want to stay with you and grandma."

I can vaguely remember feeling panicked by a thought that I was going to have to leave them and live in a palace faraway, like in my bedtime story.

"You're a pretend princess for today... see, you have a crown."

She laughed her joyful laugh: it gently broke into many pieces that felt like sunbeams that warmed me. She hugged me and stroked my hair.

"I want to play on the swing," I said excitedly. I wriggled free from her embrace.

Unusually there was still a solitary swing and a seesaw in our local park. The metal chains and posts remained. The war effort required the dismantling and donation of any unnecessary metallic items to make aircraft and battleships.

"Come on then, big girl, but you must hold on tightly or you will fall off," she instructed as she stood up and hauled me up with one hand.

I raced over to the suspended wooden seat that was imperceptibly swaying in a soft breeze. The noise of the chain links clanking together gave away the very subtle movement. Mum picked me up and placed me on the seat, worn smooth by hundreds, perhaps thousands, of pairs of children's legs on it over the years.

"Hold on tight now," she reminded me.

Standing behind me, she pushed the bottom edge of the wooden seat away from her body. I rose and flew, then dropped back down to flow in reverse. The breeze whistled in my ears and on my face. I have a picture in my mind of squealing, "Push me higher, I'm a bird."

"That's high enough for you miss, when you're older and can swing yourself, you can go as high as you like."

By now the weather had changed, the clouds covered the sun and the wind against my body felt chilly.

"Come on now, Marianne, it's looking like rain... we'd better get our things together and go home. I told your grandma that we would be back by three o'clock anyway. I have to go to work tonight."

"No! One more push, please Mummy," I pleaded.

"Alright, just one and then you'll have to slow down and get off, anyway that little boy there is waiting for his turn on the swing."

And true to her word, that was all she pushed again, just once more.

"Right Marianne, hold tight and let it slow down, I'll just pick our things up."

The voice behind me faded. Like a kite that has lost its updraft, the swing slowed down, and I stopped flying. I must have misjudged the height of the sway as it moved forward again. I let go and stepped down from the wooden seat. There was no ground under my feet, I had stepped on to fresh air. The next thing I was aware of was bright red blood flowing down from my knee, heading towards my white ankle socks. I had banged my head, and I cried.

"Mummy!"

"Marianne," she screamed, dropped the blanket and the bag on the ground and ran to the crumpled heap of a child that I must have been on the ground.

"What on earth happened? Oh! Your knee is bleeding. I told you not to let go of the swing... how did you fall off?" She looked alarmed.

"She got off before it had stopped, silly girl," the lady with the little boy piped up.

"See Thomas, that's why I tell you to wait for it to stop before you can get off or else you'll get hurt like the little girl."

Mum was kneeling beside me. In the gap of air that was between us, I could feel the tension in her body: her protectiveness rose to the surface.

"Thank you for your kind concern, I'm sure my daughter will be alright when I get her home, and no thank you, I don't need any help."

Thomas had already climbed up on the probably still warm wooden platform.

Mum helped me up, but I couldn't bear any weight on my right knee.

"Ow! Ow! Mum it hurts, stop the red stuff."

"Oh Marianne... I'll have to carry you, just stay there while I get our things."

Returning to me, she scooped me up and kissed me on the cheek. My salty tears were stinging my cheeks as I hung on tightly, my arms reaching around her neck.

"Don't forget Sammy," I sobbed.

She walked briskly while my knee throbbed. I could feel the cold blood trickling slowly down my leg. My sock was wet.

Arriving home, she took me into the kitchen through the back door. Grandma had heard the commotion and hurried down the stairs, which was something she always told me not to do.

Mum dropped our belongings on the floor, placing me gently on the end of the drainer next to the sink. She uncurled my arms from around her neck, then took off my shoes and socks. The right sock was bright red. Then she rotated my legs and feet and placed them into the sink.

"Now let's have a look at this knee, shall we? Marianne please stop crying – I will not hurt you; you've already done that for yourself."

"What in heaven's name is all the noise about?"

Grandma entered the room with an old duster in her hand. Still she cleaned our windows despite the gummed brown paper, about 3 inches wide, stuck to the inside of all our windows in a criss-cross pattern. This was to prevent shards of glass flying into the rooms in the event of a bomb blast. The dust, rubble, and destruction of the war was on the battlefields of Europe and the streets of the UK.

"She must have let go of the swing and fell off it before it'd stopped."

"That will teach you, won't it? But that cut looks deep Valérie, move out of the way, let me have a look."

Mum poured lukewarm water into a basin, mixing it with a tiny measure of the last precious bottle of Dettol we had, then bathed my knee. The white tinged water stung my wound, and I whimpered. Once it was clean, she applied some pressure to the wound to stem the bleeding. I sensed they exchanged silent, anxious looks above my head.

"Did she fall on some glass, Val? It's a deep cut."

"I didn't notice any, but I was too shocked to look to be honest."

"Right, let's put a bandage on it. And if the bleeding doesn't stop, we'll have to get Dr Lawson to have a look at it."

"I don't want to!" I said emphatically.

"Marianne, I'm not saying you will have to... just if it doesn't stop."

Grandma retrieved a bandage from the kitchen drawer and dressed my knee.

"There, that's better. Now Valérie put the kettle on."

Mum did as she was told. This distraction had stopped my crying. I giggled.

"What's funny, Marianne?" She was relieved that my tears had ceased.

"Grandma tells you what to do and you tell me what to do and then I tell Sammy what to do. So... we're all in charge."

"That's about the measure of it."

Mum laughed as she grinned at me; her face washed with pride. Tenderly, she lifted me from the sink and sat me in her lap. She hugged me tightly and stroked my face.

"Promise me you'll be brave if I am not here... if you're scared, be like a tiger, fierce and not like a princess with a crown. We all have to face frightening things Marianne, it's part of life. I truly hope that you will face them with courage."

"I promise Mummy," I murmured, unsure what I had promised. They were big words for me to understand. I hugged Sammy and closed my eyes. I think I drifted into a sleep.

As I remembered these incidents after all those years, there seemed to be an absence of any male relatives: a father, whoever he might be, my grandpa Philippe. I involuntarily touched the scar, the raised lesion on my right knee. It is still an uneven, bruised area.

Eventually I got up with a weariness in my thoughts and body. Nothing seemed to evoke any reminiscence from the past that would unlock the mystery that had become my mum and the unknown man. I went to the bathroom, splashed my face and took a glass of water back to bed. I'd opened the door to my childhood recollections, and I couldn't seem to close it again.

19

Valérie

SOE training June 1943

A week later, the bone shaking military truck approached the impressive gates of the private estate and the stately home contained within it. Once cleared through the security checkpoint, it lurched to a stop at the end of the long drive outside the main entrance. Here the olive green vehicle discharged its cargo of new recruits at the foot of the stone steps. The four men and two women stood there and gazed around at their new surroundings.

Valérie wondered who this magnificent property had belonged to, before being requisitioned for its new role of a training school. The grounds stretched as far as the eye could see, with wooded areas to each side. She did not know the location of the house but guessed that they had travelled for about an hour and a half from Southampton station to get there. The driver had ordered them to travel in silence.

Inside the grand entrance hall, the officer in charge took their identity papers and ration cards from them.

"Well, who do we have here then?" A stocky Scot looking rather more official than his rank allowed questioned them. He ran a pencil down his list on a worn clipboard.

"Because it is courtesy, we'll have ladies first on our roll call, so that's Bouchard and Grieves."

Valérie and the other woman from her journey replied simultaneously, "Yes Sir."

"And so you four must be Lawrence, Morris, Russell and Slater-Jones then: unless one of you is in disguise as Bouchard or Grieves!" He laughed at his own joke.

Then he paired them up: Valérie was to share with the pretty, diminutive auburn-haired woman. She was a few years older than her appearance would suggest. Once shown to their shared room, he allowed them half an hour to unpack the few belongings they could bring with them.

"Hello there, I'm Eleanor." Her roommate had a friendly, open smile as she extended a slender and perfectly manicured hand to Valérie.

"I'm pleased to meet you Eleanor, I'm Valérie."

They shook hands.

"Which bed would you prefer? The one next to the window or the other one? I don't have a preference, so you take which one suits you best."

Valérie chose the one furthest from the window, placed her small suitcase on top of the standard issue rough grey and green striped blanket. She opened the clasps on it and lifted the lid. A small involuntary gasp escaped from her mouth.

"Are you alright, Valérie?"

"Yes… thank you, I'm fine. My things have moved about in my suit-case and my photograph is on top of my clothes now."

Her voice quietened as she gently lifted the photo of Marianne out and tenderly placed it on the bedside locker. She felt her heart ache and knew it would not stop until she held the little girl in her arms again.

Valérie looked up at Eleanor and noticed a softness in her face that comforted her.

"Who is the child? Is it your daughter?" Eleanor stepped closer and stroked her arm.

"Yes."

Valérie simply could say nothing else to this compassionate woman, and so she turned away, removed the few remaining items from the suitcase and deposited them in the drawers and wardrobe.

"You have had to make a tough decision to leave her."

"I don't really know whether I had a decision to make at all: we are here because we want this war to end and some people believe we can help to make that happen. I want this war to end so that our children can grow up with peace, not death and bombs and fear… Marianne, my little girl, is being looked after by my family, although some days it's hard to tell who is looking after who, she seems older than her four years. Do you think that war does this to children? Teaches them far too young about loss?" She knew it was a rhetorical question, but one she felt she could speak out loud to her roommate.

"I... I lost my two boys, my twins and my husband – in an air raid... they were all unlucky that day... the boys were being evacuated the next day, to somewhere in Devon, they were so excited about it... they thought they were going on a big adventure. They were innocent in all of this."

Valérie crossed the room and put her arm around Eleanor's shoulder and felt her shudder, a painful reaction to her memories. She marvelled at how peculiar it was that war could do this to strangers – unite them on a common feeling or a shared experience within minutes of meeting one another. Before the war she was certain that both of them would have been far more reticent about expressing feelings, grief, loss to a person they didn't know.

Eleanor took hold of Valérie's other hand in a natural and comforting way.

"We're doing the right thing being here, I know it... we have to make a difference for our children, and their children... now come on, we'd better get a move on, we don't want to be late for our first briefing do we? Heaven knows what the punishment will be."

The new recruits assembled in the old dining room, waiting for the instructor to arrive. In the once splendidly decorated room Valérie noticed the grey dusty outlines where artworks had lined the walls. Presumably, they were now in safe keeping in a vault somewhere. The heavy gold brocade curtains reached the floor and there was a small fire in the ornate stone fireplace. She looked around at the other members of their group. The four men appeared to be wary of the two women and huddled together for safety. Valérie approached them and greeted them.

"Hello… we're just saying that we weren't told that we would train with women, are you sure you're in the right room?" enquired one of them with a public school accent.

"Yes, I'm sure that we're in the correct place. This is the old dining room, isn't it?"

Valérie was trying her best to keep an annoyed sarcasm from her voice. Eleanor turned from the large window that framed an exquisite view of the grounds and woods that stretched beyond the house. She joined the group.

"Yes, we're definitely in the right room, here to do our bit for the war effort like you chaps… typing letters and posting telegrams and well, oh, you know, things like that… so what do you expect to be learning here Mr?"

She gently, imperceptibly nudged Valérie's left arm. Valérie held back a smirk. She liked this friendly, cheeky and unexpected ally the more time she spent with her.

"Lawrence – Frank Lawrence. And you are?"

The instructor entered the room and interrupted any further introductions. He invited them all to take a seat as he removed files and papers from his battered brown leather briefcase. Once arranged, he looked up, cleared his throat, looking across the row of new recruits from left to right.

"Good morning, welcome to training school. First, let's get one thing quite clear before we proceed - you have all passed the initial assessments and tests over the last four days in London. And so you are all deemed to have the potential to undertake the work required. You are all here to undertake the same training. We make no distinction between male and female abilities. Should you unfortunately find yourself captured or arrested by the enemy, they will not care whether you are a man or woman. Do I make myself clear?"

The short stocky man before them was a contradiction, his soft Welsh accent was at odds with the message he delivered. The stark comment hung heavy in the air for a moment and then settled on their shoulders.

"Second, I will be responsible for you during the weeks you are here. Please do not let me down. My name is Staff Sergeant Collins."

Valérie and Eleanor glanced at one another, exchanging a smile. Both intuitively knew that their instructor had deliberately made his first remark to the men in their group.

"Where you end up being sent and what you end up doing will be different for each one of you. But we will equip you with the skills and some tricks to help you keep yourself safe on your mission... or at the very least evade capture. So I suggest you pay full attention to all lessons. Listen and learn."

The instructor picked up a set of typed notes and checked that they were in the correct order.

"This is the most important part of your training. You will, therefore, in your own interest, be subject to strict security rules. The general security precautions are a) you may not leave these grounds during the course unless accompanied or specially instructed to do so, b) you must never, ever, disclose to anyone that you have been at this training school and c) you must not act as though you recognise anyone you have met here if you meet them later on elsewhere, except on official business."

Valérie felt a chill of isolation and loneliness at the thought of this. She could not just leave and visit Marianne and Winnie.

"May I ask a question, Sir? Are we allowed to write letters home while we are here?" She suspected that if she needed to know the answer to this, then the others did too.

"Good question Valérie – yes, but all of your correspondence leaving here will clear through the usual security protocols and censored, where necessary."

She felt some small comfort in this and promised herself that she would write a weekly letter home.

"And that leads me nicely into covering the practical details of security here concerning valuables including money, your identity documents. We will also cover weapons, incoming and outgoing mail, telegrams and telephone calls by the end of today." Staff Sergeant Collins placed the notes back on the desk.

"Is that understood? Ask if anything at all isn't clear – I would remind and urge you all to understand that it is your responsibility to comply with everything we teach you over the coming weeks."

The expected chorus of "Yes, Sir" made him smile as he picked up a fresh set of notes.

"First, let me bid you a proper welcome. I hope you will enjoy your course here and that you find it helpful. Remember – and I will keep repeating it – this training could save your life when you're out in the field... Now let's get to work. The purpose of the Organisation to which you and I belong is the fourth arm of modern warfare."

Valérie listened intently as she tried to take in all the introductory talk. The repetition of the themes was apparent: enemy, damage, destruction, disruption to communications, interrupting production, resources, undermine morale, help to the Resistance, sabotage.

Eventually his voice stopped. He scanned their faces.

"Right, I think that is enough information for one day, so let us reconvene at 0700 hours sharp on the rear lawn. We will be outdoors tomorrow – come rain, hail or shine. Dinner will be available from 1800 hours in the dining room in the South Wing across the Grand Hallway. You will take all your meals there."

The group of recruits moved and stretched in their seats. Valérie looked at her watch. It was 5.30pm already.

"But there is one final yet vital thing to say: we do not consider ourselves to be spies in the conventional sense of the word. We are subversives and our objectives are to conduct sabotage and reconnaissance in a variety of ways through the means of subversion. And this subversion, properly applied, is one of the most potent weapons one can use."

The following morning was grey, wet and drizzly as they set off across the estate grounds on the first of many three mile runs. On their return, the unexpected substantial breakfast was very welcome.

Valérie found the first week physically and mentally demanding with long days of classroom lessons and outdoor training. Her previous role had not prepared her for this assault on her body. Her tired and aching muscles then had to cope with gruelling sessions learning the basics of weapons handling, unarmed combat, elementary demolitions, map reading, field craft and basic signalling and the use of radio communications. Each day ended with Valérie and Eleanor collapsing on to their beds with mental and physical exhaustion, depending which activity had filled their day. They both suspected that their fellow trainees were experiencing the same fatigue, although they did not say, at least not in front of their female counterparts.

The second week was a repeat of the first, but the trainees did not receive a typed timetable now. They did not know what activity to expect next. Valérie guessed that this was a deliberate ploy and was part of their trainer's method of assessment – so that they could observe how the recruits reacted to the unpredictable and unknown itinerary.

On the Saturday afternoon at the end of their second week, they gathered for a debrief in a downstairs room. It had once been a study and was now their classroom. That morning they had completed a practical explosives and demolition session at the far side of the estate grounds, in an old quarry site. Valérie was glad to be indoors again. It had rained all day. She wondered how long they would have to sit in their sodden clothes. She was becoming colder by the minute but knew this was intentional too. Their trainers were introducing more and more uncomfortable situations as the days passed in order to acclimatise them to the harsh conditions they could encounter once they were in the field in France.

She felt miserable and homesick as she looked around at her colleagues. She wondered whether they felt the same depth of missing their families as she did. Had she done the right thing after all? Staff Sergeant Collins entered the room and interrupted her thoughts of Marianne and Winnie at home in their warm back kitchen.

"Good afternoon, everyone. Now I hear that your last exercise had varying degrees of success... isn't that correct Mr Lawrence? A home-made explosive device will not explode without the use of a detonator, will it? Well done to the rest of you, the ladies in particular."

The instructor smirked, and Valérie was sure that Frank Lawrence reddened a little as it exposed his basic error to the group. Eleanor nudged her arm. It had become their secret sign of encouragement to each other.

After a half an hour of questions and answer session, Valérie yawned, and Collins noticed.

"Right, if no one has any further questions we shall finish for the day... no, right, fine? Get changed into dry clothes."

"I'll be glad to Sir. Just one question – what time do we begin tomorrow morning, Sir?" asked Eleanor.

"Oh, that reminds me, I have some important news for you all... you have a free day tomorrow, to do with as you wish... I suggest you make the most of it and get some rest. The next two weeks are going to get tougher."

Back in their room, Valérie and Eleanor grinned at each other as the prospect of an entire day to themselves loomed.

20

Valérie

The letter home

Valérie and Eleanor were grateful to have slept beyond the 5.00am daily alarm of the past fourteen days. The Sunday morning of their rare free day dawned.

"What are you going to do today?" Valérie asked Eleanor as she propped herself up in bed. Her sore muscles delighted in the warmth of the blankets pulled around her. She pushed the thought of stepping into the cold bathroom with the lukewarm trickle to wash in from her mind for now.

"I don't know – it's an unexpected turn of events isn't it? I might just stay here and sleep!" she laughed.

"No one could blame us, could they? It's been a hard couple of weeks… but I have a feeling that we'll still be under observation today, to see how we spend our time."

"Do you really think so Val?"

"Yes, I'm fairly sure we will – have you noticed the bald man at the next table when we have our meals? And then he seems to hang about in the games room later."

"No! oh blimey Val, I've failed the observation tests then haven't I?"

"Don't be daft, course you haven't failed... I don't think we're supposed to notice him, he's there to watch us and make sure that there's no fraternising in our group... we're the only one with women in it, and it wouldn't do for any of the gentlemen to become sweet on us or form any romantic attachments, now would it?"

"I really hadn't thought of that – not that any of them have caught my eye, anyway."

"Are you sure about that, Eleanor Grieves? I've seen you looking at Roy Slater-Jones... he has a certain appeal, if you like that upper class sort, full of their own self-confidence and privileged background." Valérie teased her friend.

"Oh dear, was I that obvious? Don't you think he has a certain charm? But he's not really my type, and anyway – who would take me on - a widow?"

They laughed, cherishing the friendship and shared experience of loss within the comfort and security of their temporary bedroom.

"Be careful Eleanor, you really shouldn't get attached to our colleagues here... and that means you and me too, I suppose... the future is uncertain for us, but it is the path that we've chosen."

"I know, I won't."

The silence of Sunday morning surrounded them for a few minutes, and both women were grateful for the ease of their company together.

"So what will you do today, Val?" Eleanor said as she swung her legs out of bed.

"I'm going to write a letter home for Marianne and then find a quiet spot in the garden and read... if I had been at home I would have been knitting something for her."

"Good plan – now I'm going to use the bathroom first, you don't look like you're getting up yet."

And with that Eleanor left the room, hugging her towel and wash bag to her chest.

Valérie was alone with her thoughts. And the knowledge that her letter home was going to be full of half-truths and outright lies. The smokescreen of secrecy continued to surround her.

Dearest Mum and my darling Marianne,

I have been here for two weeks now and I'm learning lots of new things and there are lots of tests. At first I found the amount of information was overwhelming, but I'm getting through it all. I will probably move to the operational room next week and start training some of the other girls to use the new equipment.

They are all friendly and come from all different parts of the country. There is one Scottish girl that has a really strong accent and I can't understand her most of the time. Six of us share a dormitory. It's comfortable enough and we're warm, but I do miss my bed at home. Sleeping in bunks is uncomfortable.

Sometimes it can be noisy and I crave some peace and quiet to myself. I would rather be at home with you.

We are being fed well, our meals are in the canteen and some days there is even a choice of main meal or puddings.

If you see Celia, please say hello and tell her I am well.

I miss you both very much and I hope I'll be able to come home soon. I also hope that you are being good for your grandma Marianne. Make sure she helps you around the house, Mum, at the very least, by putting her toys away.

Anyway, I have to go now, I'm back on duty in half an hour.

With lots of love and kisses for you both and a big special cuddle for Marianne,

From,

Val and Mum xxxx

21

Valérie

Training resumes

In the blink of an eye, Monday morning arrived again and the freedom of their restful Sunday faded. They assembled as usual in the makeshift classroom.

"So what do you ladies think we'll be doing this week?"

Valérie studied the smooth Slater-Jones as he addressed his comment directly to Eleanor. She hoped he wasn't flattering her new friend. She had tried to warn her.

"I think we'll be learning more radio signals – codes, ciphers that kind of stuff," Valérie jumped in as quick as a flash as Eleanor went to reply.

"We're bound to be covering more about recognition of the enemy... uniforms, weapons, and so on," Russell chipped in.

Frank Lawrence joined them. "And parachute landings in the dark. Anyone ever jumped before?"

No one had, and Valérie noted Frank's smug look. "There's nothing to it, just remember to count and land correctly. Might be tougher for you girls though if they send you over in a dress."

Eleanor felt Valérie's arm tap against hers as they recognised his first attempt of the day at his usual conceited prejudice. Valérie's patience with Frank was wearing thin. She had noticed that Morris and Russell seemed to tolerate his irritating manner while Slater-Jones was so full of his own class superiority and didn't really notice anyone beneath him unless they had a use to him.

Further speculation about field craft, transport and false papers followed as Staff Sergeant Collins entered the room.

"Good morning everyone, we're here again."

"Good morning, Sir," they sang in reply. His lilting Welsh accent had somehow encouraged that over the previous weeks.

"I trust you enjoyed your day off everyone and took my advice. You will need all your powers of concentration in this next two-week block of training. Now I won't lie to you, it will be particularly challenging and some of you may not make it through to the last phase."

"How many usually pass the course, Sir?" Frank asked.

"About 50%, sometimes up to 60% if it's a talented group."

Collins let the statistic hang in the air.

"Right, let's get started then. For the next two weeks, every exercise is a simulation of a situation you could and probably will find yourself in when you're in the field. We will grade you individually on the success or otherwise of the completion of each task. The grading is a pass or a fail, nothing more complicated than that. Too many fails will show that you will die if you behave or react in the same manner when in France. Is that clear?"

The chorus of, "Yes, Sir" was more subdued than usual.

Valérie felt a shiver grow the length of her spine. The reality of the potential danger formed as a dry constriction in her throat. She had not left Marianne and Winnie and undertaken this training in order to fail. Her determination to help bring peace in the world closer was a solid certainty within the core of her being. Valérie had enjoyed each new challenge and revelled in each new skill as she learned it. She particularly excelled in communications, and she was very aware of how desperate the French were for skilled radio operators.

"Now, I will issue your new identity to each of you and your cover story. Memorise it. Then you will go to the library and locate a wooden crate with your name on it. Remove all the contents from your box and take it with you. You must prepare to leave for the field in an hour exactly. You must not, I repeat, must not take any belongings from your room that would identify you to the enemy. Take items of clothing as you will not be returning here for several nights. Is that clear?"

The "Yes, Sir" chorus reduced in volume again. A recognition that things were about to become serious dawned on them.

Two hours later, Valérie again found herself in the back of the truck that had collected them from the station two weeks ago. They were under orders for complete silence. Collins had blindfolded them all. She had safely concealed the pistol in her jacket pocket. The truck tossed them about as it travelled over an uneven surface. Was it a rutted field? The smell of diesel seeped in through the floor. Her destination was unknown.

It was a long three days and nights later when the truck pulled up again outside the manor house steps. The six bedraggled trainees clambered down from its rear compartment. Their bodies were stiff and aching. Valérie was sore from the rigours of the field exercise. Their orders were to debrief at 19.00 hours.

Valérie and Eleanor linked arms. They slowly climbed the grand staircase to their room on the second floor in silence. Once inside the room, Eleanor slumped on to her bed.

"Are you alright? You look exhausted, Eleanor. Why don't you have a bath and leave the water in for me?"

"Oh, Val... wasn't that tough? I ended up sleeping under a bush last night, I lost my bearings to the rendezvous point... I didn't sleep, I was so cold, I could hear animals making noises... I'm not sure I'm going to be up to scratch for this."

Valérie sat next to her on the bed. She put her arm around her friend. Eleanor looked so lost and shocked after their field simulation of an exposure of their address and identity that meant they must go on the run to find a contact they could trust.

"It certainly tested us. Did you see Slater-Jones face when we picked him up at the side of that road? He looked shell-shocked."

They held each other for a moment of comfort. Then Eleanor stood up.

"Look at the state of me! I'm being stupid, I know I can read a map – I just had the blasted thing upside down, that's all! But please don't tell the men Val," she grinned.

They laughed so hard that their eyes watered, a shared moment of absurdity in what had been a cold and frightening situation. Their eyes had been opened to what they would face in the future.

"Go on, get in that bathroom now Eleanor Grieves, or do I have to take you there myself?"

Eleanor's back disappeared out of the room as Valérie realised that those were exactly the words she would have said to Marianne. She missed her so much.

And then the fourth week of training was soon upon them. As they assembled for the Wednesday morning session, Valérie noticed that Frank Lawrence was absent.

"Where is Frank this morning? He's going to be late... and I don't fancy doing an extra lap of the parkland as a penalty if he is."

The other men in their group looked at each other, assessing whether they could trust Valérie and Eleanor with information that they obviously held.

"He won't be coming with us today... they send agents who struggle here on to another training school... they call it the 'cooler.' I've heard that it's somewhere near Inverlair, up in Invernesshire," Colin Russell informed them.

"Oh, I see," said Valérie. Frank must have had too many fail grades in the previous week's assessments. It was her turn to give Eleanor an unnoticeable nudge.

Before they could speculate any further as to the reasons for Frank's departure from the training course, their instructor entered the room. They all stood to attention.

"Good morning, and a fine one it is too. Please, sit down ladies and gentlemen."

It was a sparkling summer morning, one of those days that starts with colours that are extra bright and clear. He did not remark on Frank's absence from the group.

"Right... you all need to pack your belongings and be ready to leave in an hour. There will be transport waiting outside the main doors to take you to your next phase of training."

The group of five glanced at each other.

"Are we allowed to ask where this is, Sir?" enquired Valérie, mischievously.

"You may ask, Miss Bouchard - but you will not be told." Again he recognised the sharp mind she had showed in their training exercises and classes. He had observed the knack she had of exploiting any opportunity that came her way to get any information she could.

"As we suspected... I presume you will return our ID papers to us, Sir," said Eleanor.

"Don't worry Eleanor, they will go safely to your next location," advised their instructor. "The next part of your training is to prepare you for duties with F Section of the SOE."

22

Marianne

In London

I felt exhausted again as Janet and I headed to London. Sleep was
still evading me, but I didn't want to let Janet down. I knew she was
looking forward to our day out.

After a morning trawling the archives at Kew, I had several pages
of notes about the WAAF and a couple of somewhat intriguing and
unexpected references to Saint Girons. The historical details about
the organisation and role of the WAAF was comprehensive, and the
wide-ranging roles that women had undertaken within it amazed
me. I felt like I had a better understanding of the skills my mum
must have had as a radio listener. The references to Saint Girons were
another matter entirely – they were vague and lacked any context.
I gleaned it was an important town for the French Resistance and
that, possibly, there'd been some British help to the Resistants in that
region of France. But there was nothing specific for me to go on. I
couldn't find any references or connections between the WAAF and
Saint Girons.

Leaving the noisy, claustrophobic Westminster Underground station,
Janet and I weaved our way through the busy lunchtime crowds. The
busyness of the city never stopped: everyone rushing here and there,
the blasts from black cab taxis horns, the red buses queuing and

crawling, the cyclists weaving precariously in and out of the traffic. The air tasted of transport fumes as we reached Parliament Square tube station.

"Well, let's see what the War Museum can tell us about the WAAF. If I could just find something that links it to Saint Girons, then it might help me figure out how she came to be in France in 1943. I still can't work it out, Janet. They stationed her on the south coast. There's a missing link between them somewhere."

"Well, if you're asking me I think it's Jacques... come on Marianne, you've got to admit that the more you look at the photograph the more it resembles him. Don't you think?"

"I honestly don't know; I only spoke with him for a few minutes and his face is disappearing from my memory."

There was a whoosh of air through the underground tunnel before the train pulled up to the platform. We stepped into an eerily empty carriage. It trundled along the tracks through the darkness. Five stops later, we left the Lambeth Road station and walked to the museum.

"There you go ladies: your tickets and information booklets. And here's a guide to the layout of the exhibitions. We have a temporary exhibition on the third floor about the Secret Service during World War II that's fascinating."

"Thank you. I'm actually looking for information about the WAAF. My mother was in it in 1943, actually."

"Have a look at that exhibition. And you're in luck today – the Curator is in the gallery. Look out for Christine, she might be able to help you."

"We will, thanks."

Janet and I agreed we weren't overly interested in the aircraft and Word War I exhibitions so we visited the café for a cup of coffee and a slice of cake then used the washroom facilities.

After showing our tickets to the bored nail chewing young man at the door, we entered the empty third-floor gallery. London's Friday lunchtime crowds obviously didn't venture here for their entertainment. My eyes adjusted to the dimmed lights of the aisles of the exhibits enclosed in their glass cases. The distant commentary of a wartime newsreel interrupted the quietness. I vaguely remembered that distinct over-pronounced southern county dialect from my childhood when grandma listened to the BBC Home Service news bulletins about the progress, or otherwise, of the war.

Janet and I wandered along the rows of artefacts. Uniforms, many objects used by the Secret Service from cameras to pens, silk maps, posters, photographs. Many adaptations to everyday items that were used discreetly when agents were in the field. Incongruously there were identity cards for the people who worked in these clandestine sections of military organisations and Government departments. The information panels did not state whether the photo identity cards were the owner's true identity or their alias.

I scoured the information boards on the Secret Intelligence Service, the forerunner of MI5, and the Special Operations Executive for any mention of a WAAF connection.

"Marianne, quick - come here and look at this." Janet beckoned me with an amazed look on her face.

I walked past the remaining glass cases into an open area with half a dozen seats placed in front of a large projector screen playing old newsreel footage.

"Oh, you've missed it, it's on a loop, you'll have to wait for it to come back round again, it'll be back up in a minute."

"What am I watching for?"

"It's like a home recording on an old cine camera, it's after this news bulletin."

I waited patiently until the screen pictures changed to a new title: French Resistance.

"This is it, look closely Marianne."

I saw grainy, jumpy, stilted images of what looked like a village square appear on the screen. The colour-faded, moving pictures showed people going about their business. It was as if the camera was slowly, deliberately panning around the buildings and filming the people. I noticed that the camera operator focused on German soldiers around the square, recording each one for a few seconds. Then the panoramic view moved around to the entrance to what looked like a civic building draped with a swastika, a town hall perhaps.

"Watch after the town hall, it's about here."

The camera panned around to the left and a sandy coloured stone built church with an elegant spire came into view. The camera stopped at the grey stone steps leading to the entrance. And there I saw a young couple laughing as they stood close together on the steps. I gasped loudly at the shock of the familiarity of the scene.

"Oh my word Janet, it can't be! That's, that's mum, that's my photograph, but it's a film... how? How on earth? I don't understand."

And then the camera panned further to the left and concentrated briefly on two SS soldiers with rifles slung over their shoulders, both smoking casually in the sunshine. Then suddenly it was black: the lens cap snapped over the viewing lens sharply. I was shocked to think that she had been so close to the cruel Occupiers of my grandpas country. I realised my hands were shaking.

"That's what I thought. But how is it possible? Are you ok Marianne? You've gone deathly pale; I think you should sit down."

It felt like an eternity as we waited for the four-minute loop of film to repeat itself. In that short section of film again, I stared intently at the few seconds of footage of the couple. I saw my mother as a vivacious and vibrant woman in the company of a good-looking young man. Both were full of life, playful even. But was the tall, almost elegant man Jacques? There was certainly a confident and assured air about him. I felt the sting of tears behind my eyes at the sight of my mum after all these years.

I glanced around as I heard footsteps approaching from behind. A woman joined us.

"Hello, are you enjoying the exhibition? You've got it all to yourself this afternoon, but then again museums aren't everyone's cup of tea on a Friday afternoon, most people prefer the pub these days."

"Err, yes, are you?" The chatty woman had interfered with my concentration on the screen.

"I'm probably a bit too close to make that judgement, seeing as I'm the Curator," said the cheerful woman.

"Aah, are you Christine? The lady in the ticket office said you were here today."

"Yes, I'd love to hear what you think of the displays if you've got time."

"Well, actually I'm glad you're here, Christine. The old film going round here, may I ask, where did you get the piece in the French village square from please?"

I felt lightheaded and quite detached from my body with disbelief. I put my hand on Janet's arm to steady myself.

"Oh, I don't know from the top of my head, I'm sorry, but I will have a record of the source or who we've loaned it from. We borrow items from lots of other collections and war museums around Europe for things like this. I'll be able to look it up and let you know if you give me your phone number. Are you ok? I really think you should sit down; you don't look too well."

"Thank you, I think I will."

"I'll fetch you a glass of water, stay there."

A few moments later, I felt revived by the drink.

"Would it be possible to find out who the footage belongs to? It could help me no end, I hope. Sorry, I should've said, believe it or not but that bit of film is of my mother, I can't believe it to be honest... we came to find out some information about the WAAF. She was in it during the war. But I didn't know she had been in France in the war until a couple of weeks ago. And it makes little sense because I always thought that she had been at an RAF station at the south coast when she died in 1943."

"And the other thing is that my friend has recently discovered a photograph, and it's a still of part of that film. But we don't know is who the man is with Valérie. She was Marianne's mother. Isn't that amazing?"

"What? You have a photograph still of the film? Well, I never. What a coincidence for you. I tell you what, seeing as we're so quiet I'll have a look at my records for you now."

A few minutes later Christine returned with an A4 spiral-bound notebook.

"Let's go through to the foyer area outside the gallery, there are some comfy seats and it's lighter out there."

As we followed her through the exhibition, Janet linked my arm. As always, I could feel her concern for me. I smiled and said, "I'll be ok, don't worry."

"Rightio ladies, let me see, it looks like that piece of film is on loan to us by a French museum, The Musée de l'Ordre de la Libération. It's in Paris. We asked them for help with French Resistance artefacts and information."

This mystery deepened, and I was trying to think clearly about the clues I had so far. I tried to picture my dining room information wall again.

"That's interesting... Libération, did you say? I can tell you they shot the film in Saint Girons in France, if that's any help to you. My photograph has two names, and the place scribbled on the back of it."

My mind was a whirr of images as I tried to recall what Mike had said about Jacques. Hadn't he said that Jacques received a Libération medal?

"Ah, I see. I wonder?" Christine looked pensive, "I'm just wondering if the film reel has any details on it that might help you."

"What? You have the actual film reel here? In London?"

"Yes, so that we could take a digital copy of it to put it with others, together in a loop that will play onto the screen all day. Come on, let's go down into our basement and see our Gary. He's our archivist and looks after all the items that we borrow. Let's take the lift."

Down in the basement Christine asked us to sign in the staff register with her as we entered what was usually a non-visitor area through a yellow security door. We followed her between rows of grey metal shelving containing hundreds of labelled boxes. At the end of the row, she knocked on a door and entered a small windowless office.

"Gary, there you are, glad you're in residence today."

"Oh hi Christine, come in, won't you? What can I do for you?"

"Well, something quite unusual actually. Could you dig out one of the donor exhibit pieces from the Secret Service show for me, please? It's a cine reel of film, came in from a French museum."

"Yes, sure." Gary clicked around on his computer and after a few moments his face lit up, "Got it, is it part of the footage that we've spliced for the loop film on the big screen?"

"Yes," I replied as I realised I was holding my breath in anticipation.

"Let me just get it for you, I'll be back in a jiffy."

My look of astonishment at the unexpected turn of events of the afternoon made Janet laugh out loud.

"See, I told you that finding the photo was exciting Marianne, but who could have guessed we'd have uncovered this though? It's definitely like something from a book or a film."

"It's an astounding coincidence for sure, but it sort of doesn't tell me anything I don't already know, does it? It doesn't tell me what mum was doing in France and it doesn't tell me for sure that the man is Jacques Allard, does it?"

"So you think that the man in the picture was Jacques Allard?" asked Christine.

"Possibly, I'd never heard of him until my grandmother's funeral a few weeks back. He turned up there, he'd sent gorgeous flowers, arranged in blue with white and red like the French flag. Then he disappeared. It was all odd...."

"Blimey!"

"Here we are," said Gary, entering his office again. He placed a tissue paper wrapped circular object on his desk. He pulled on a pair of cotton gloves, then carefully unwrapped the flimsy paper to reveal a silver tin. The lid unscrewed and inside was a small cine reel of film, about three inches in diameter. Gary carefully removed the film reel.

Christine then fished a pair of identical cotton gloves from her pocket and picked up the tin lid. She took a magnifying glass from her pocket and looked at the lid closely, scanning it slowly through the lens.

"Mmm, they shot the film on a Revere Eight model cine camera. I'm fairly sure they were an American model... do you know Gary?"

He was peering at the film reel under an eyeglass too.

"Yes, manufactured in Chicago, I believe. They took Kodachrome film reels, 8mm. It was a handheld manual camera. A pretty snazzy thing in its day with a leather carrying case. Now they're sought after by interior designer types for upmarket bars, galleries, if you like that sort of place."

I got the impression that Gary was a proper pint in a real pub kind of guy and not one who frequented London City's trendy wine bars. I watched as Christine turned the lid over and looked closely at it. She frowned.

"There're the remains of some sort of label inside the tin, something written on it but I can't quite make it out... aah, if I turn it round it says Albert then underneath Henri. Henri with an 'i' not a 'y'."

"Is there any information on the film reel, Gary?" I asked, praying silently that there was.

"No, sorry."

It disappointed me that neither referred to Jacques Allard. My heart sank as I was no nearer finding out who he was. I took a small note-pad from my bag and jotted the name Albert Henri down in it.

"Thank you both for your detective work, I really appreciate it. I'm not sure if it gives me any more to go on, but it may be a clue to finding out who Jacques Allard is."

"You're welcome, it's not every day a visitor has a direct association with an exhibit and especially one they didn't know about before they walked in our doors." Christine beamed at the thought.

"I wonder, could I push my luck and ask something else?"

"Fire away, it is amazing what information and artefacts we hold in storage here," said Gary.

"Is there any way to find out whether the WAAF were active in France? I'm trying to work out how my mother came to be in France in 1943 and filmed with an American-made camera in Saint Girons. Or did the WAAF have connections to the USA at all? Is that a possibility?"

"Let's see what we can find out for you, Marianne. Leave your phone number with Gary and we'll call you if we find anything. I'll get a research intern on it on Monday. What was your mother's name, by the way? We might find something in records on her, y'never know."

"Valérie Bouchard."

"But on the back of the photo Marianne has at home it says Lucille," Janet added.

"Now that is interesting indeed!" exclaimed Christine, "She had a real French name, but it suggests to me she possibly had false papers in France. I don't know whether you've thought about this Marianne – but this is an exhibition about the Secret Service during the war."

Her statement hung in the warm air of the small room as the other three occupants looked at me.

"What? You think my mum could have been under cover there? A spy? I hadn't even thought of that as a possibility."

The day before we were due to fly out to Carcassonne, the phone didn't stop ringing. I was busy packing and allowed the answerphone to pick up the call. I recognised Mike Walters' voice immediately as he spoke to the tape recorder.

"I guess you're not in bonny lass, call me back when you can pl-"

I snatched the phone up in the middle of his please. "Mike, I'm here," I said as I glanced down at an orange dress in my hand with impatience. I wandered into my dining room investigation headquarters.

"There you are, I was hopin' to catch you, I remembered you were going to France at the end of the month. Sorry about this but I've had an update on your Frenchman – it seems the updated local records show he's moved, to a new address, but they don't show where he's gone to, unfortunately."

"Oh, bloody hell! We're flying to France tomorrow as well. Oh, damn it!" My exasperation made Mike laugh.

"Sorry to be the bearer of bad news... if I hear anything about a new address, I'll let you know straightaway."

"Thanks, Mike. I'm just disappointed that's all."

"Obviously, you sound just like you used to on a real bank job."

"Do I? Oh dear! This is important to me, Mike – it's turned into a personal investigation, and you know me – I need to know the answers. Anyway, just a thought, while I've got you, can you have a look for me and see how many people live in Clara-Villerach please?"

"Yeh, sure, coming right up... now let's see... last year's census returns say 160 residents. Why?"

"I'm just wondering whether it's worth visiting, anyway. If it's a small village, then everyone will know everyone else. Somebody might know where the disappearing Jacques has moved to."

"Mmm it's probably worth a shot – local intelligence, nosey neighbours and all that – they've proved invaluable to us over the years."

"Thanks again, Mike. I'd best finish my packing or I'll be sharing Janet's clothes and they're really not my style."

"And sorry, I've had no luck at all on tracing any elderly gentlemen with the name Albert Henri. Not a squeak, I'm afraid."

"Thanks for trying anyway, Mike. This is still off the record if you can keep it that way please I'll be grateful."

"No problem pet, you have a great time, drink plenty of vino and let me know if you track him down."

"Thanks, I will. Bye."

I returned to the bedroom with the dress and folded it into the suitcase. Ten minutes later the phone rang again. Exasperated at another interruption, I grabbed the phone.

"Hello, Marianne speaking," came out far more aggressively than I'd intended.

"Oh, err, hello it's Gary, at the War Museum, if now's not a good time I can call you back later."

"No, now's fine. I'm sorry Gary, the phone keeps ringing and I'm trying to pack to go to France tomorrow, that's all."

"It was just to give you an update, really. I can't find any direct connection between the WAAF and the French town. But what I have found is quite interesting, I'd say... there was an organisation with the unfortunate acronym, believe it or not, of FANY. It stood for the First Aid Nursing Yeomanry, and it was a cover section or front to move some WAAF women into other roles. Seems like it was a secretive organisation. Whatever it transferred them there to do was a secret... so there's no actual records here that I can find. But what is interesting, it also appears that some of these women ended up in the Special Operations Executive, the SOE. Again because that was secret work there's few records about it... I can't find any that show that your mother was in it, but that's not to say she wasn't... sorry I couldn't find much else for you."

"Gary, believe me, I can't thank you enough for what you and Christine have done for me and my search. I've jotted those names down and I'll add them to my list."

"Good luck with your search and if you find anything, just to get in touch with us and we'll see if we can help. I'd best let you get on with your packing, have a safe trip. Bye."

And with that information, I had yet another piece of a riddle that didn't fit together with anything else that made sense. It was as though I had two different jigsaw puzzle pieces mixed up in the same box: one was an incomplete picture of mum's role in the WAAF and in the war overall and the other was Jacques Allard and just what was his connection to her. The picture of the mystery wasn't becoming any clearer as I heard Janet come in the back door.

"What's up?"

She stood by my side and peered at the information board on the wall as I stepped back from writing the additional information on it under the Who? Section.

"Gary from the museum has just called and given me a bit of information he's found about the WAAF, but he couldn't find anything about them being in Saint Girons."

"Aah, and I'm guessing that it doesn't shed light on anything by the look on your face."

I laughed, "You know me well, Janet. And Mike rang before him. To say that Jacques Allard isn't at the address I had for him, he seems to have moved. That'll explain why he hasn't answered my letter... just my luck, eh?"

"Oh, Marianne, that's rubbish news, so we won't be going there after seeing your cousins then... I'll cancel the hotel."

"No, leave it booked Janet, we'll go anyway and see if his neighbours know where he's moved to, it's worth a shot. We're not too far away, anyway."

"Ok if that's what you want to do."

"In the meantime, put the kettle on will you please flower? I'm ready for a cuppa and it might just spur me on to get this flipping packing finished. Have you done yours?"

"Yep, all done, I was up with the larks, I'm really excited about our trip. That's why I popped in - I've been and picked up our currency from the travel agents as well - and I picked up some cakes to have with our morning coffee."

"Thanks, Janet. I've just got some bits and pieces left to put in my case, it'll take two minutes."

23

Marianne

France

By the following evening, pleasantly tired from the flight and the driving, we reached my cousin Marie-Clare's house. The address she had given me did not divulge that it was a fairy tale chateau that she and her husband Pierre had restored before he died suddenly two years ago. It was the last time I had seen her and my French family. Then she had merely said that they had restored a house in the countryside.

Widowed Marie-Clare had wondered how she could maintain the property. One weekend she made the house available to a local family for a wedding. From that a business venture had grown, so that it was a popular wedding venue in the area and with British summer holiday makers too.

After an evening meal accompanied by a bottle of superb red wine, we retired with coffee and a fine cognac to the terrace. The sunset was changing colour by the minute from orange to gold to red. After the upset of the events of the last couple of months, I felt a calm settle within me. Perhaps it was reconnecting with family and being close to my grandpas area that settled me.

"Now Marianne I have spoken with Simone and Alain and we agree it makes sense that you stay here for the duration of your holiday. I have lots of space and unfortunately Alain has to go away on business next week. But we have arranged a family party on Saturday. So, they will all come here with their families. We will celebrate being together and remember our Tante Winnie and Oncle Philippe with you. And we will remember your Tante Helene and Oncle Joseph too."

"That is so kind of you, if you're sure we're not putting you to any trouble we would love to stay here with you, wouldn't we, Janet?"

"Yes, please. This is a little slice of heaven: you have a wonderful home and the gardens and the view are inspirational. I'm going to sketch this tomorrow if you don't mind."

"No, not at all. Many people say that when they stay here. I'm happy to have you both here, I know there are always people here but they are strangers, visitors... it feels different when my guests are family. Thank you for coming. It is an enormous home just for me, and I miss Pierre still. Now tell me about the man you are trying to trace here."

We talked late into the night about the recent events and discoveries since the funeral. And we drank a little too much brandy. And as is the way of these things, Marie-Clare reminisced about our childhoods and the occasions after the war when grandma bought me to see my grandpa's and my uncle Joseph's family.

"Marie-Clare, do you remember your parents ever mentioning Jacques Allard or Albert Henri when you were growing up? I'm wondering whether they knew your father, Uncle Joseph... or even if something related them to him or Aunt Helene?"

"No, I'm afraid I don't, I've never heard those names until tonight. But ask Simone and Alain when they come on Saturday, they may recognise them."

"Oh, it's all very frustrating! I know there's something to see, but it's not clear, it's as if I'm looking at the complete story of mum, France and Jacques through an opaque window where I can see the shadows behind it but can't see anything clearly. Perhaps I don't find out what the actual picture is and I'm wasting my time and effort trying to track him down. I felt like giving up yesterday after Mike called me."

Janet knew I felt despondent by the turn of events. The alcohol wasn't helping by inviting a melancholy into my heart. Being here with my family was a reminder of the past. These relatives had known grandma, and by association this reminded me of mum through the haze of the mix of wine and brandy.

I still had a longing to have mum there, present, and alive during life's big events. This had not faded over the years. I recalled that her absence was bigger than a person-shaped hole as each one cropped up. My school prize giving, later life university graduation, my ill-fated and short-lived marriage, the miscarriage. Then there was the year of looking after grandma after her operation and the gruelling chemotherapy treatment. When was that? About twenty-five years ago now. I recollected thinking at the time how much easier it would have been to have a helping hand and someone to share the worry with. These events were lonely and frightening without my mother at my side, where she should have been.

"I'm sure we'll find something out when we visit Jacques village, Marianne. We can't give up now, we've come this far. You'll see, it'll all slot into place."

Janet's eternal optimism coaxed me from my maudlin memories. The need to sleep and rest from my unanswered questions overwhelmed me.

"Time for bed methinks, it's been a long day."

Saturday arrived, and around lunchtime the tranquillity of the previous days at Marie Claire's chateau shattered. The place burst loudly into life with Alain and Simone and their collection of daughters, sons, some grandchildren and two dogs.

Every member of the family smothered me with kisses and hugs, and much to Janet's delight, so was she. Her drawing and sketching of the grown-ups as caricatures mesmerised the children. And so we set up an informal art class on the terrace. The parents' relief was palpable and gave us all a chance to catch up and talk.

It was a warm, hazy day and slightly humid. The lawn to the front of the house was a perfect summer green, while the meadow to the rear was awash with thousands of flower heads of red, blue, yellow, white and lavender. Butterflies floated and dipped in the slight breeze, accompanied by the buzzing of bees. Marie-Clare's decision to hold an outdoor buffet and barbeque was perfect, especially as I had concerns about how much work this would be. But I need not have worried.

"I have ordered the caterers from the village. They will deal with the food and the drinks, local families who cater when we have weddings here. No work for us to do Marianne, we just have to enjoy being together."

As I looked around, it was a family gathering on a perfect afternoon. I had not felt this relaxed for a long time, and it felt like the decision to come here was the right one. No matter what the outcome.

However, conversations with Alain and Simone did not uncover any further connections between the mystery French men and mum and grandma. Neither of them had heard any mention of Jacques or Albert as they grew up. It disappointed me; I had truly hoped there might have been a tiny thread that linked them and us. A thread that I could have tugged and it would have unravelled the mystery.

24

Valérie

A new training location

The journey was hot, noisy and thoroughly uncomfortable in the back of the personnel truck. The seats were wooden benches, and Eleanor and Valérie improvised a cushion to sit on out of their extra clothing from their suitcases. As the summer heat increased, their driver stopped once to allow them to stretch their legs. He rolled up the tarpaulin at the back of their transport to allow some air in. The trainees could only see what was behind them, receding into the distance, rather than the direction they were heading in.

As evening fell, they were travelling through country lanes. Around dusk they passed some large buildings that looked like a collection of large sheds. In the fading light, Valérie could make out the shape of aircraft hangars behind them. Ten minutes later, the noisy vehicle stopped outside an Edwardian house. The driver turned the engine off. The silence of the English countryside on a summer evening invaded the truck.

"Thank God we've stopped at last, they could have at least sent us here on a train, even if it had been in second or third class," Slater-Jones complained.

A tall and wiry man appeared at the back of the truck and appraised them.

"You made it then, not the most pleasant of journeys, but you'll experience worse than this soon. Now make your way to your rooms and get yourselves settled in. And we do not allow you gentlemen in the ladies' quarters under any circumstances. Then head downstairs to the canteen area for cooks delicious stew. You'll soon get used to it. We seem to have a variation of it every day."

A jovial Yorkshireman delivered the instructions. One by one they jumped down from the back of the vehicle with their suitcases.

"And where do we need to report for training Sir? And what time?" Valérie asked.

"Good question – 07.00 hours here and not a minute later, we have no room here for sleepy heads and late comers mind. I'm Flight Sergeant Young, by the way. Don't be late."

He looked at each of his new group of trainees, returning his gaze back to Valérie. He made a mental note that she was the recruit that had asked and had wanted to know their schedule beyond their next meal and a bed tonight. That skill will stand her in good stead in the future, he hoped.

Valérie opened the door to their room, grateful to be sharing with her friend again. This time they found themselves in more basic accommodation in another unnamed location.

"Welcome to your new home," Eleanor grinned. They looked around the room, stripped bare of any decoration and with three single beds arranged along the longest wall. Only two had a pillow and grey blankets neatly folded at the foot of them. The bedroom was functional and had a feeling of being makeshift, an interim stop before its occupants moved on to somewhere else.

"At least there are curtains at the windows... and it doesn't look like we're sharing with any other girls, does it?"

"And look – we've got an inside bathroom, well a sink and a lavatory at any rate... Val, it's positive luxury to what some poor souls in London are living in, let's thank our lucky stars."

"Yes, you're right, we should be grateful for this... there are still hundreds, thousands having to shelter in the underground and makeshift homes in cellars. And I'm glad that Marianne and my mother are relatively safe, bombing seems to have stopped nearby."

"I won't bother unpacking – we'll only be here temporarily, I think."

Twenty minutes later, they headed downstairs to the canteen for their meal. This room had once been a grand ballroom and rather incongruously its sparkling chandelier still lit the room.

"I wonder what's on the menu tonight?" Valérie said as she closed the door behind her.

At the serving station, a rosy faced cook greeted them, "Hello my dears, you're new girls I can tell – now you're lucky and you've got a choice tonight – eggs or stew, which will it be?"

The look on Eleanor's face meant that neither looked appetising. "What would you recommend?"

"Oh, the stew is more filling, you'll be needing your strength here," said the cook.

"I'll have the same," said Valérie.

She served up two generous portions and added a spoonful of potatoes to the side.

"There you go, my dears... Have you jumped with a parachute before girls?" she quizzed as she stirred the dish of anaemic-looking scrambled eggs made from the powdered then reconstituted version that was the nearest thing available now.

"No, we haven't."

"They say it's in the way you land... do you want some pudding tonight? Only rice left, I'm afraid."

"Yes please, we'll both have some." Eleanor's eyes lit up at the prospect.

They looked around the room and saw that Russell and Morris were already eating their meals. They all sat together on the wooden benches in comfortable silence now. After spending the last month in each other's company, they were familiar with each other's quirks and moods.

"So, what do you think has happened to Frank?" asked Albert Morris, now affectionately known as Bertie, to them. He was the quiet man in the group.

"I think we probably can assume that he's failed... despite all his bravado and bluff," said Valérie between mouthfuls of the unsweetened rice pudding.

As they ate the tasteless dessert, Valérie noticed Eleanor's paleness.

"Are you alright, Eleanor?"

"Yeah... no, parachutes? I'm terrified of heights."

"Oh, you poor thing - just do what I do and follow the instructions... it can't be that difficult, can it? After all, people are being dropped by parachute every day."

"Yeh... I suppose you're right – the RAF wouldn't exist if there weren't bombs to drop and people to parachute behind enemy lines, would they?"

"You'll be fine, Len," said Slater-Jones as he sat down to join them.

"Don't call me Len please, it makes me sound like a man, my name is Eleanor, how many times do I have to tell you?"

Valérie realised that Slater-Jones felt a gulf in the difference between his background and theirs, more so than the rest of the group, as he had no one from his class and education to relate to. His nickname for Eleanor was his way of trying to assimilate into their group and perhaps endear himself to them. And perhaps to Eleanor, too.

"I'm sorry, I'm didn't mean to offend you... we've all become friends over the last few weeks, and it's the first time in a long while since I've had some real friends."

"So, have any of you gentlemen parachute jumped before?" Valérie asked.

All three of them shook their heads.

"If it's any consolation Eleanor, I'm terrified of heights too. I don't know how I thought I was going to get to France, but I didn't think I'd have to jump out of a plane to do it," Bertie reassured her, ever the pacifier in the group.

25

Valérie

Practical parachute jumping

The following morning Flight Sergeant Young noted the time that each trainee arrived on duty.

"Mmm, Slater-Jones, you cut that rather fine - by thirteen seconds I see. But you haven't let me down, so that bodes well." He checked his paperwork again and nodded.

"Right off to work then, let's learn how to jump out of an aeroplane. It's a ten-minute walk to the hangars. Head straight down the track and turn right on to the airfield – it's shed number two. I'll meet you there." And with that Flight Sergeant Young jumped into a two-seater van and sped off.

"Come on Eleanor, best foot forward, you'll feel much better about this after today, I'm sure." Valérie tried to reassure her – or was she really trying to put her own mind at ease? The thought that by the end of today she would know how to jump out of an aircraft in darkness over enemy territory struck her as absurd. And by the end of the week, they would expect her to do it with confidence. Now that was seeming a little foolish as she was a mother and a daughter, not a man. Men jumped from aircraft and fought the war. Or at least they had done until now. She hardly recognised herself these recent weeks.

"Does anyone have a clue where this place is?" Colin Russell interrupted her thoughts.

"We're at Ringway, somewhere near Manchester," said Slater-Jones, "I asked the cook last night. It's the RAF Parachute Training School. The house we're in is a holding base for trainees like us. She looked rather sad when she said she never saw trainees like us again once we've completed our training... she never knows whether they live or die."

The sombre thought hit home as they approached shed number two. Next to it were other hangars and a large repair workshop. Behind these was the airfield. An almighty roar as a Lancaster took off diverted their attention from the danger they were to face soon.

Flight Sergeant Young was waiting for them in front of the cavernous open fronted structure.

"It took you twelve minutes to walk here, I expect it to take you eleven minutes tomorrow. That minute could be vital when you're in the field. It could mean the difference between life and death." His cheery, good humoured manner had disappeared as he walked away from them. "Follow me, ladies and gentlemen," was his sharp order, loud and clear.

By lunch time they had received instruction on jumping from a one storey building height platform and learned the correct technique of landing. By the end of the day, they were outside in heavy rain and flashes of lightning. The previous day's summer heat had created the conditions for a thunderstorm.

"Do you need a hand with your parachute, Valérie? If you roll it up rather than trying to fold it, you'll find it easier to bring it under control. Roll it up as tightly as you can... that's it. Remember that you'll need to do this in minimum time when you land in the field."

"No Sir, I'll get the hang of it... after all, there won't be anyone to help me when I land for real will there? Mind you, wrestling parachute silk in the rain is pretty exhausting Sir!"

Young watched her as she began the task again and meticulously rolled up the white silk into a tight roll. Then she stopped and seemed to think for a couple of moments. She removed a hairgrip and slid it on to the roll of fabric to stop it unravelling again. He nodded his approval, impressed again by the practicality of this female recruit. He moved along the line of recruits and assessed their progress. The conditions were dismal now, but could be realistic on their mission. They would need to dig undiscoverable holes in the ground to conceal weapons and other equipment. And then be able to cover up the fact that they had dug a hole at all. On their landing drop night they should work in clear weather, moonlight being a requisite requirement of the drop taking place. Young thought to himself that it was all good practice for them.

They were glad to walk swiftly back to their accommodation that evening and remove their damp and muddy clothes.

After the usual dinner of stew, Valérie, Eleanor, Bertie and Colin gathered in the old library and relaxed into the comfortable sofas there. Bertie had his head in a book that he had borrowed from the well-stocked shelves. Eleanor crocheted and Valérie knitted with yarns, hook and needles given to them by the cook. Colin played a game of patience that the others all knew he cheated at. No one knew where Slater-Jones was. Valérie looked up as a stranger entered the room.

"Hello there," said the softly spoken upper class man with sand coloured hair as he approached their group. "I thought I'd find you here."

"And you did," grinned Valérie, "Would you like to join us? A parachute recruit, are you?"

"Yes, and no... I shall only take a few minutes of your free time if I may, I appreciate how precious it is while you're here... I'm Frank Muir, the photographer here. Now if you could step into the next door lounge, one at a time please, I will take your photographs for your new identity papers and documents that you will need. Obviously, the photos need to be in civilian clothing... you'll all be fine in what you're wearing now. Ladies, you may apply some lipstick if you wish, but nothing too obvious or garish please."

Slater-Jones entered the room and joined them.

"And tomorrow I shall take film footage of your final training jumps, for our records and for your final assessment. You may wish to apply stage make up for that, although the film is for training classes and not at the local Gaumont cinema I'm afraid." He winked at Eleanor.

Then on Friday morning Flight Sergeant Young informed them they were to spend the day in their makeshift classroom and that there would be no further jumping practice.

"Today you will sit your final assessment papers and subject to the required standards being met, we hope to release you into the world of subversion against the enemy soon."

Valérie's heart stopped for the briefest of moments. The time for leaving seemed to approach her quicker than she felt ready for.

She sensed that time had speeded up over the last few days and she would soon – sooner than she would like – be saying goodbye to these friends and colleagues and their amiable company since Frank Lawrence had disappeared.

"Now, these tests must be under silent conditions. No conferring please. You have an hour to complete all the sections. You may begin at 09.30 hours precisely."

After a brief break with a thin empty sandwich and weak tea lunch, the afternoon session began. An unnamed officer individually interviewed them in the lounge. He briefed them on their new identity papers and cover story, then sent them away to memorise it. They were to wait for further instructions in the canteen.

An hour later Flight Sargent Young stood in the doorway and called out Valérie's name. He told her to report straightaway to a low-roofed red brick outbuilding at the back of the house. As she approached it, she noticed it had no windows. Valérie knocked as she entered the dank and dim room, but she could see no one there. Abruptly, an officer dressed in a German SS uniform approached her from the shadows and shouted an order to another person behind her. She was shocked as this unseen person roughly grabbed her elbows behind her. He fastened tight metal handcuffs to her wrists. The faceless person shoved her forward. Then there was silence as she heard him step outside and slam the door.

She tried to calm her nerves by taking several deep breaths, but still her mind could not comprehend the powerless situation she found herself in. What on earth was happening? She was standing before an imposing fair haired man in a Waffen SS uniform. She must stay calm.

"What are you doing here? Who sent you? The English? What is your name? Where are your papers? Where are you going to? Tell me - I NEED ANSWERS NOW," the man roared at her. He held up a thin cane in his right hand and brought it and his pock-marked face close to hers.

She could smell something stale on his breath. Was it cigarettes or was it coffee? He slowly walked around her and stroked her hair as he passed her back. Valérie recoiled and tried to focus her attention on his questions. Adrenalin rushed around her body. She could feel it in her blood, and finally it rested in her common sense. The relief of a realisation that this was a role play flooded her brain. It was a test of her ability to stick to her cover story and identity. She must recite her details and answer his questions with conviction.

"I am."

She knew her voice sounded shaky, and so she feigned a cough and cleared her throat.

"Here are my papers, I am going to the bakers to fetch bread, if there is any left."

Once more the room was in silence after Valérie answered his questions.

And then the man stepped forward from the wall he had stood against and nodded to her.

"Well done, Miss Bouchard, you did very well there – you answered all the questions in a roundabout way and convincingly too. You will do well to remember this exercise - it could save your life. Now, let's get those handcuffs off you, shall we?"

"Yes, please – I don't know if I should call you Sir or not," she said as she looked him directly in the eyes.

He laughed and then his face turned serious, "You must not under any circumstances at all tell anyone what happened here when you return to the house. Do I make myself clear?"

"Yes, Sir," Valérie replied. She stepped outside and took a gulp of fresh air and prepared herself to return to her fellow trainees, as if nothing so brutal had happened.

The late afternoon session went over quickly with reminders about security of cover, alertness, inconspicuousness, discretion, discipline and planning for an emergency.

Finally Flight Sergeant Young dismissed them with a "Good luck and stay safe, please. And alive. We would very much like it if you returned to SOE for a debrief in the future."

Flight Sergeant Young had informed the novice agents that their training was complete and they had all successfully passed. The feelings of relief and apprehension competed in Valérie's heart and mind. They were to return to their rooms and prepare to leave tomorrow morning. He reminded them they were not to tell anyone about where they had been and what they had been doing over the previous months. Their official story was that they had been helping to train new radio operators and listeners to use some new, more advanced equipment.

Valérie was tired and had a headache as she returned to their room. She lay down on the bed and curled her knees up to her chest, just like Marianne did, and pulled the rough blanket over her. She closed her eyes and drifted into thoughts of home and holding Marianne close to her. But more than that, she longed to be close to her own mother, dear Winnie. And to be told everything will work out for the best.

Eleanor entered the room half an hour later and Valérie opened her eyes. She saw her friend in a subdued manner, her shoulders hunched and worry lightly brushed across her face. Eleanor seemed too young to face what was coming and yet so much older than her years after her tragic loss.

Valérie stretched out and yawned. "Well, this is it...it seems like we're finished here."

"Who knows where we will be tomorrow?"

"Oh Eleanor, we are doing the right thing... aren't we?"

"We've made it this far... some of our group didn't... we have to do what we must do to end this bloody war. I'm sick and tired of it. Surely it won't be much longer?"

26

Marianne

Clara-Villerach, France

A week later, after an emotional farewell to Marie-Clare with promises of keeping in touch and seeing other more often, we took a pleasant drive towards Clara-Villerach. Leaving the Ariege region, we headed east towards the Pyrénées-Orientales region. I drove and Janet navigated. Eventually we were on the D35 road and approaching the village centre in our hired red Citroen Xsara. I parked alongside the pretty central village green just before lunchtime. It was quiet except for a dog barking. We climbed and stretched ourselves out of the car.

In the distance there were green and grey hills, and behind them the high mountains of the Pyrenean border with northern Spain and the Catalan area. The air was clear and fresh as we walked along a main street in search of a bistro or café for some refreshment in the afternoon heat.

The café owner insisted we sat under the shade of the canopy on the pavement outside his shop. He served us with coffee and glasses of iced water and then returned with a selection of tiny fresh warm pastries. Janet and I were happy to watch the world go by for a while as parents collected their small children from school. Then a few more people came out after the usual French extended lunch time. The longer I sat in the cool shade, the more nervous I became of finding out where Jacques might be. I was unsure why.

As the owner replenished our glasses, I asked if he could direct us to the Rue des Acacias. He hesitated. Few visitors passed through, and this was a genuinely small community where people watched out for each other.

"And what is your business there?" he quizzed me.

"I am looking for a man who lived there, I believe he has moved. I will ask his neighbours if they know where he has moved to."

"And who is it you're in search of please?"

"An elderly gentleman called Jacques Allard – do you know him by any chance?"

"Aah! Jacques, yes, he lives in the house next door to my Maman. You are a friend of Jacques, yes? Come - I will show you where."

"But how can he live next door to your mother? I was told he has moved from the street, that makes little sense."

"No madam, he still lives in that road. He has moved to a bigger downstairs house there. A house without the stairs."

"Oh, I see. So what number does he live in now?"

Janet squeezed my hand as we looked at each other in astonishment.

"Maman lives at 26 and Jacques is in the next house with the red front door."

"Thank you, there is no need to take us there, I shall find it. Now, how much do we owe you for our drinks please?"

"Nothing, you are a friend of Jacques, so I am happy to have served you. He is a good man who has done many good things."

"If you insist. Again, thank you."

As Janet drove us this time towards the Rue des Acacias address, I became apprehensive again.

"Janet, stop a minute please... I'm not sure I'm doing the right thing at all now. What if Jacques is there but doesn't want to speak to me? Is it rude just to turn up uninvited in France? I don't know... and what if he speaks to me and I find out something I would rather not have known? Ignorance is bliss, as they say."

Even after all my investigations and wanting to find out his connection to mum, the reality of being here and what it might mean unnerved me.

"Marianne listen, you have come this far you can't give up now. But if you're not sure, why don't you sleep on it, eh? We can come back tomorrow. Let's head to our hotel." Always the practical one, Janet felt my discomfort with going on any further today.

"Would you mind Janet? I'm not sure I'm ready to do this yet. And..."

After a silence, Janet intruded on my thoughts that had been troubling me for a couple of days.

"And what? What's the matter, Marianne? Has something happened that you haven't told me about?"

"No, nothing's happened... but I think I've spotted something in the information I've gathered and I don't know what it means, it's confused me even more... I'll show you when we get to the hotel."

We checked in. I showered first, then unpacked while Janet sang tunelessly in the gleaming white bathroom. I lifted a folder containing some details I'd gathered together before we left home from the bottom of my suitcase. Placing it on to the coffee table between two armchairs, I opened it again. The hotel manager had upgraded our room to a small suite at a bargain rate when we enquired about staying at least an extra couple of nights. The extra space was welcome. We had become used to the luxurious and generous rooms of Marie-Clare's home.

I took out the snippets of information that had disturbed me when I noticed the inconsistency. I knew I would not have even looked at the bits and pieces in front of me now if I hadn't dropped the folder and its content when I was repacking my suitcase this morning.

Janet entered the room at the same time as there was a knock on the door.

"Room service, madame."

Wrapped in a towel, she invited the server to put the tray on the side. His admiring look made me smile.

She then deposited a large Martini in my hand.

"Merci, looks like you made an impression on the waiter there."

"Cheers, Marianne. You looked like you needed a drink."

"Un apéritif, splendide," I replied, taking a sip of the chilled aromatic herby liquid.

"So, what's on your mind, Marianne? You've been quiet all day."

I placed the elegant cocktail glass on a side table, pushed the photograph of mum and Claude and then the ageing 1943 telegram across the glass topped coffee table toward Janet.

"Look at them closely again – look at the difference."

Janet frowned as she picked up both items. One was words and the other was a picture. "I'm not sure what you mean, what difference?"

"Turn the photo over, look at it again... I just can't believe I've missed a tiny detail like that. The number of times I've looked at these things - I must have lost my touch. It's probably time to retire..."

Janet stared at the faded words on the reverse and then looked at the telegraph. Her eyes moved back and forth between them as though she was watching a high speed tennis match. Then her brown eyes widened as she saw it.

"But how can that be? How can the telegram date be before the photo?"

"I have absolutely no idea unless it's a mistake or..."

"Oh my God, Marianne. What if?"

"I know it's a fantastical thought Janet... but could my mum still be alive? Is it possible?"

The thought of it was too big to contemplate as a serious suggestion, or even as a possibility of the truth. My mind was a whirr of noise. I could not accept that all that I had held dear and true through my childhood, indeed my life, was a lie, an untruth. I drained the Martini from the glass, then Janet did the same.

"I think we need some more of these and let's just get room service. You look exhausted, Marianne."

I nodded in agreement, contentedly being cared for, to not have to think about trivial things. Curled up in the armchair with a cushion, I closed my eyes, trying to comfort and calm myself from these unwanted thoughts.

Janet replaced the phone.

"Right, that's all sorted. Now… let's be practical, Marianne. It makes no sense that they delivered an official telegram to Winnie to say your mother was dead when she was clearly still alive."

"Mmm. I know that but the date on the photograph may be wrong. But the other possibility is that she, she…"

I could not voice my other thought, the enormity was too painful to hold in my heart.

"What Marianne? What?"

"That… that, oh Janet! Did she leave me behind and go to France to be with the man in the picture? That she abandoned me… she didn't want me."

"No! I don't buy that for a minute, Marianne, not from how Winnie spoke about your mum. Why? Why would she do that?"

"Love? Lust? Money? Blackmail? I don't know."

"No Marianne, I still don't think that's an explanation. To just disappear like that and not contact her mother or you ever again, that doesn't feel right somehow. Women don't do that, just leave a child behind without a reason..."

"Perhaps... but what if she did Janet? What if the guy is Jacques, and she's been with him all these years? And it could explain why he turned up at the funeral – because mum couldn't bring herself to come and face me."

"Now you're in the realms of fantasy, Marianne!" My reasoning clearly exasperated Janet. The room service knock at the door intervened in our discussion.

"It's not beyond the realm of possibility, people disappear and assume new lives Janet – I've made a career of trying to track some of them down, so I know what I'm talking about." Half-formed thoughts swirled around in my mind; I rejected each of them. It seemed a preposterous proposition.

"Yeh, I know that and I can see that there's some mileage in your theory, but my gut instinct tells me that's not the case with your mum."

"Not even if the man is my dad?"

I hadn't intended that thought to escape from the confines of my head and became a spoken, tangible expression of my confusion. The apéritif had loosened my tongue unintentionally.

"Oh, Marianne... is that a possibility? I didn't think you knew who he was."

"That's just it – I don't!" I shouted at her.

I stood up and walked to the window. The hills in the distance peered back at me as the sun set behind them. An orange and blue sky glow filled the room. The calm solidity of the landscape washed over me and I felt contrite. Janet was my loyal friend and was on this journey of discovery with me.

"I'm sorry, Janet, I don't mean to take it out on you. I'm just so frustrated because I'm - because I haven't got the answers, that's all. And this has just added to the mystery of who mum was."

"I know, it's such a shock for you. Come on, sit down and have a bite to eat."

I turned from the window and knew that whatever the next few days brought would be a new truth, a new reality in my previously ordered world.

"Grandma always said that my dad was someone in the RAF. Mum never told her his name. She said that mum said he wasn't important if he couldn't accept the responsibility of fatherhood. I remember once overhearing grandma and mum whispering about something, I was only young, about a man waiting for her when she came out of work and something about him being a married man... I've carried that with me ever since, I suppose I've sort of convinced myself that my father didn't want me."

"But I still don't think that was true of your mum."

"Perhaps. I really don't know what to think anymore, Janet."

"Right, we need a plan. So - we'll find Jacques' house tomorrow and talk to him. He must know something that will put your mind at rest."

"That's what I'm afraid of... that I'll be taking the lid off Pandora's box and letting out the secrets of the past that are better left there."

"Well, if you don't want to, then we don't have to go. We can check out in the morning and see if we can alter our return flights and you'll be home tomorrow evening – none the wiser. And we've had a delightful time along the way. It's your choice Marianne, you decide."

I finished my drink, took a fresh Martini from the tray and picked at some olives and breadsticks. Janet was right. I'd come this far following a trail that led to Jacques. And he held the truth.

"I know you're right, as usual. Let's try to talk to him and see what he knows. It feels like I'm on the threshold of something."

"You are Marianne."

"A toast, I think... to the truth, whatever that might be."

27

Valérie

Leaving for France in autumn 1943

The next morning, Valérie and Eleanor exited the station and walked through the streets of London. The scarred landscape of buildings were like skeletons, the bare scorched bones of homes, shops, offices. Other dwellings were like washed up seashells on the beach – an outer frame with burnt out emptiness inside. The grey dust had settled on to every surface.

They strolled towards their destination for what they expected to be their last instructions. They walked in silence, but their thoughts were loud in their minds: they may never see one another again. Valérie was conscious she had no luggage with her. They had forbidden them to take any personal possessions or anything that would identify them as British. Her heart weighed heavily at the thought of not being able to carry a picture of her dear Marianne.

"We've got plenty of time so let's stop and treat ourselves to a cup of tea, it might be the last decent one we can get for a while, I'll pay," said Valérie.

"Ooh, y'never know – we might get a cake or a biscuit to go with it, we could share one."

Eleanor's enthusiasm as always was welcome to Valérie. She knew she would miss her dearly.

"There's a little place around the next corner here, my father used to take me there."

Valérie opened the door to Gladys' Tea Rooms. The bell over the door rang a cheery, welcoming chime. The warm, foggy atmosphere of steamy windows, baking and cigarettes enveloped them as they found a table in the corner. Valérie noticed several seated customers tipped their heads to them, recognising their WAAF uniforms. Uniforms and identities to be discarded by the end of the day, no doubt.

The aroma from the kitchen behind the counter wafted about the busy little shop. Eleanor smiled at Valérie as they perused the short menu.

"This place always smells delicious... it reminds me of when Papa used to bring me here as a child when he used to come up to town."

Valérie could still remember the unique smell of her hot buttered toast that he would always buy for her.

A young woman in Women's Royal Naval Service uniform at the next table drained her mug and stubbed out her cigarette. The white spiral of smoke and the smell of used tobacco mingled together, then wafted across their table. The girl, for that is what she appeared to be to Valérie, gave them a wide smile as she left.

Little did these strangers know that Valérie and Eleanor's last few weeks of training had included being taught how to kill, if – perhaps when – necessary. How ordinary their steaming mugs of tea and a freshly baked Chelsea bun seemed in comparison. The women grinned at each other and savoured both the aroma and the moment together.

"Thank you, Valérie, this is a real luxury. Now let's enjoy it and make a promise that we will return here one day after the war and we'll have a whole bun each... and some toast. And it will be my treat next time."

Valérie reached across the table and touched her friend's hand. They had become more than that - confidantes and a strength to each other over the previous weeks of training. She smiled a wistful smile at Eleanor.

"Oh, that would be a big and uncertain promise to make, don't you think? We both know that we don't know what the future will bring... and what and where we're going to, well... we might not return," Valérie whispered.

Eleanor drained her mug of tea and wiped her mouth.

"Let's not say goodbye, Eleanor, let's both carry a hope in our hearts that we will meet again."

"Come on, we'd better get moving and report for duties unknown at Baker Street."

Vera Atkins hugged Valérie close, then stepped back and saluted her. Being saluted by a senior ranking officer felt peculiar to Valérie, even more so because she was out of WAAF uniform. They'd dressed her in second hand French branded clothing.

"Go now, the weather is perfect for tonight's drop," Vera said. She wore her trademark sheepskin lined flying jacket despite the warm autumn evening.

Valérie saluted her in return, turned and approached the aircraft steps. She did not look back, knowing that if she did, her resolve and the agonising decisions she had made would evaporate into the September evening air. She stepped forward with heavy legs and climbed the steps, following Colin Russell into the belly of the cargo plane.

They sat down as directed by the loading crew amongst the crates of supplies that were making the same journey across the Channel.

"Ok Valérie?"

"Yes, I think so Colin... I suppose we should use our cover names shouldn't we Jean Paul," she said, "Actually it quite suits you," she grinned.

He returned a nervous smile and squeezed her arm briefly. "That's the spirit, too late to turn back now, old girl, as Slater-Jones would have said."

The Lysander aircraft's engines started up and startled Valérie. Lost in her thoughts of home and Marianne, she felt the prick of tears in her eyes. The mechanical scream of the engine had a repetitive rhythm of its own, and soon the constant whirring of the propellers added to the chorus.

The aeroplane juddered and rattled as it crossed the airfield for its approach for takeoff. The rattling and shaking of the interior echoed around inside her head. She hoped that the vibration of the machine did not affect the nuts and bolts that were inspected by the engineers when it had returned from its last mission. The noise intensified to a deafening din as the engines revved and the aircraft gathered speed.

Once they were in the air, the overwhelming sounds settled: the constant drone of the aircraft told her it was transporting her to her work in France. After a while it felt quite soothing to her frayed nerves from the previous night's lack of sleep. Eleanor had said she had not slept well either. Valérie had restless dreams, and she wondered where her friend was now. The hypnotic hum comforted her while she focused her thoughts on the parachute training course at the Manchester flying school. She went through the correct jump protocol and checklist once again in her head. Then she repeated the sequence of events to herself.

Suddenly a crackly intercom voice interrupted her thoughts.

"Get ready, five minutes to drop zone, repeat five minutes to drop zone."

As she approached the aircraft door, she heard her heart pounding loudly in her ears. The wind created a cacophonous noise in her ears. She knew it would relieve her to hear the whooshing of the parachute as it opened.

She stepped forward and tried to recall her training again. Her mind went blank for a moment. What was she doing here? Surely, she should be at home with her family... a couple of deep breaths later and she refocused her mind. She checked she had a firm hold of the suitcase containing the radio transmitter. She checked her right pocket for her gun. Her training schedule now returned to her mind. Next, she checked her upper pocket for her documents. The new and false identity papers that transformed Valérie Ann Bouchard into

SOE operative Lucille Durand, from the Ariege region, a widow, and a teacher. And then she stepped forward from the aircraft.

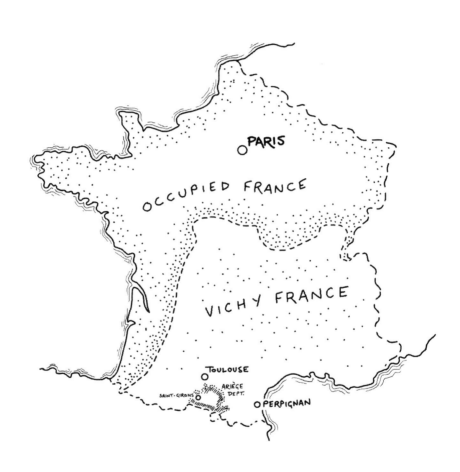

28

Valérie

France

France received many agents of different nationalities into their secret networks. As the Lysander approached the French field Valérie was unaware of the reception party that had assembled beneath her in the moonlight. They had made their way separately, silently and furtively to the edge of the field. Careful not to trip or stumble over tree roots, they were alert to all the noises of the woods to their right. They concealed themselves in the shadows of the trees. The September night air was cool and damp with the clear skies above. The silent watchers in the field knew to wear their warmest clothes, not that they had much to choose from as they headed towards 1944 and another war winter. What they had was threadbare and the temperature would drop a few degrees more while they waited. The fear of being overheard or discovered limited the reception committee to the briefest of conversation. By now they all knew their roles for each lunar routine. The requisite full moon shone down on the matt black Lysander. The RAF painted their drop aircraft to prevent the German searchlights from picking them up in the skies.

The navigator located the spot to drop the precious cargo of personnel, arms, money, supplies of food and explosives. They would help the group on the ground to continue to obstruct the German occupation. At around 1.20am, the hidden group heard a feint yet distant hum in the sky. The signals operator was nervous, on high alert, waiting for the exact time to flash a small torchlight and transmit the two coded letters to signal that it was safe to proceed. The two new agents would parachute first, and then the cargo pushed out of the plane behind them. Rarely were conditions this good: a moonlit evening with little breeze to blow the parachuted cargo off course.

The aircraft approached, low and difficult to make out in the hazy light of the moon. The signaller gave the correct all clear signs. The night went silent. As the distant engine noise approached again, the ghost like mushroom shapes began falling from the sky and drifting towards the field. This was the most dangerous and nerve-wracking of times. The reception group held their breath and continued to lurk in the shadows as the air drop landed. First the people and then the crates. The parachute clouds billowed like white fluffy forms on a summer's day. But it was not obvious which parcels were human and which were fresh supplies. They waited a minute to identify which deflating clouds gathered themselves together from the inside. Two of the shapes reduced the volume of the diaphanous mass. Once identified, some Resistants rushed forward to gather the inanimate parachutes and detach the precious cargo from them. Again wordlessly they bundled the parachutes together and disappeared in the opposite direction, manhandling the wooden crates and tarpaulin covered parcels.

Once Lucille had gathered the silk together, she looked around for the flashlight signal. She saw a tall, lean man approach her. He beckoned her to follow him into the shadowy edge of the field. He asked for their code names.

"Lucille," Valérie replied confidently in perfect French.

"Jean Paul," whispered Colin. Valérie could hear the tenseness in his voice.

The man nodded at her. The code names were correct.

"Je m'appelle Claude, bienvenue en France," the tall man replied. Again he gestured to Lucille and Jean Paul to follow him. He took Lucille's suitcase from her, a typically French chivalrous gesture. Her father would have done the same, thought Valérie. She gave him a small but grateful nod of her head, in a typically French way. There was no need to accompany it with a thank you.

After a silent twenty-minute walk through the woods alongside farm-land, they crossed over a small wooden bridge and saw a large barn in front of them. They walked past it and rounded the corner. There was a farmhouse in complete darkness. As the group reached the door, it opened from the inside. The farmer's wife Madame Chartres pulled them roughly inside. Silently, she closed the door behind her. Then she lit a single candle, and the room glowed. The dim light cast long shadows across its whitewashed walls.

"Bienvenue les amis Lucille and Jean Paul," she greeted the new arrivals and spread her arms wide.

Lucille hugged the old lady in an easy and compassionate manner. She was grateful to be concealed indoors, after the walk to get there. Jean Paul was more formal and shook the work worn woman's hand.

"Viens et mange," she invited the visitors to the wooden table to eat. A simple meal of bread with cured ham and local, thin red wine.

Lucille protested, saying they could not take their hosts food, but Madame Chartres insisted. She appealed to her husband to back her up as he entered the room. Claude reinforced their requests to partake of the food–telling them in no uncertain terms that they may not eat again for a good while as tomorrow they would travel again. With that, they sat and ate.

After their refreshments, Claude informed Lucille and Jean Paul that he would meet them at the train station the following morning. He handed train tickets to St. Girons to them. Monsieur Chartres would take them there in his van using their precious petrol. For now they must rest, try to sleep as the days ahead would tire them with the work required. Claude wished them a good night's sleep and left quietly through the rear of the farmhouse. Madame Chartres led them into a secret room in the loft. The concealed compartment contained two straw beds topped with eiderdowns and pillows. She told them she had no use for such fripperies while her two sons were fighting the German Occupiers. She would rather they gave their helpers a comfortable night than them go unused.

Jean Paul's thoughtfulness touched Lucille as he made an excuse to leave the room while she undressed. When he returned, she was asleep.

The next morning Claude met Lucille and Jean Paul at the station as arranged. Their false papers and identity cards examined and passed scrutiny by the young but stern looking German soldier. They were cautious, not wanting to arouse any suspicion, and spoke infrequently to each other. They waited for the train to pull into the station. Lucille could hear her heart beating loudly in her ears. They boarded the train and found an empty carriage, stowing away the scruffy-looking suitcases in the overhead luggage rack. It had taken London a few weeks, initially, to realise that sending the incoming agents with new suitcases drew attention to both the case and the carrier. They were incongruous with the shabby clothes that everyone wore now. The contents of these battered cases were crucial: the radio transmitter device and the delicate, invaluable glass crystals. Without them, the sets were not operational. Claude knew that the clothes of the agents all had French brand labels in. He also knew that Madame Chartres would have checked them last night. If any were not convincing, she would carefully unpick the stitching and substitute an authentic label. Like many rural French people, she had learned new skills in order to defeat the Nazi occupation; she was a dairy farmer's wife with many other talents besides milking cows. Sabotage had many disguises.

"Are Jean Paul and I going to be working together for you?" asked Lucille. She was becoming concerned that she would be. Lucille had increasing doubts about his ability to remain detached from their shared training. Some of his mannerisms stood out as 'un-French' and they worried her. He could give both of their identities away if they worked together.

Claude shook his head. "We are heading to Saint Girons, from there we will go our separate ways. Your first task is to make sure that you hide your radio set away, then to contact your network. We suspect the Germans are tracing the wireless signals more frequently, that they are listening in to most of them, so it is vital that you do not draw attention to yourselves... this is especially important. You must blend into the town, go about your daily business with ease. Be and act relaxed, but not complacent. Hopefully, there will be a bicycle available for your use, as couriers for the local network you must take messages and travel about... please take great care of it as we have great difficulty getting this transportation."

Refreshed after her night's sleep, Lucille was alert to her surroundings. She noticed that Jean Paul appeared tired. He put his head against the side of the carriage and dozed for a while. Suddenly the carriage door opened violently. The noise startled him. Claude threw him an intense look with his eyes. Lucille was frightened that he would speak in English.

"Identifikationspapiere." An overweight, middle-aged German soldier demanded their papers. A rifle was slung over his right shoulder.

They handed their papers over. They waited. It felt like an age to Lucille as he took an inordinate amount of time to inspect each set of forged documents. As he was about to pass them back, he took out Lucille's again. He considered the documents and then smirked at her. She returned a polite yet beguiling smile to him. The action repulsed Lucille, but she knew she had to be a chameleon, able to adapt to her surroundings and absorb the colours and environment she found herself in with utter plausibility. This would help her survive.

"Wohin reisen Sie?" he enquired about her journey, his voice almost challenging her to a duel.

"Saint Girons pour rendre visite à ma mère, elle est mal," she replied calmly and directly to his hooded eyes, perceiving an unspoken threat.

"Ggut, ich hoffe, sie erholt sich bald," he wished her mother well as he handed their documents back to them. He turned abruptly and left the carriage.

"Phew!" whistled Jean Paul. "That was close."

"You both handled that well, tres bien, we got away lightly, but take this as a warning, you will face tougher grilling than that from the Occupiers, especially some younger Nazis, brainwashed in the narrow-mindedness of taking away Europe's freedom. Hitler is intent on achieving this. Although I feel that the tide is now turning towards the Allies' favour."

Lucille let out a sigh and sat back in her seat. She closed her eyes. At that moment, she didn't feel so brave.

"You acted well, Lucille," said Claude.

"Merci," she replied. His encouragement calmed her nerves again. Lucille thought how ironic then that her mission posting was close to her late father's departmente. She had family in the Ariege region - cousins, aunties and uncles, although she did not know what had happened to them. No letters had arrived from them for nearly eighteen months now.

The train slowed down as it neared the bridge over the River Salat in the distance. They were about twenty minutes from their destination. Lucille glanced at Claude. She saw a look of concern glide across his face. She had a feeling of foreboding.

"Are we approaching St. Girons station?" Lucille stood up to retrieve her suitcase.

"Sit down, no, we're not there yet," Jacques ordered.

Lucille stared at him, understanding the implications of the stern statement.

"The Germans have a reason to stop the train - it could be to pick up troops or supplies... or someone's papers are not in order, or they may suspect that one of our associates has tampered with the railway tracks... whichever, please, you must stay calm." He directed his words towards Jean Paul.

The train slowed to a halt with a shudder. The silence was palpable. It felt dense, menacing, heavy. There was a thickly wooded area to the left, the tall trees seemed to have dark shadows, yet there was no sunlight. After a few minutes, the barking dogs and angry, shouting soldiers cut through the air. The ringing crack of gunfire ahead of the carriage suddenly interrupted the noises. Two bullets. Then the train creaked and groaned into life and inched forward. As it rolled slowly, Lucille saw four relatively well-dressed figures being escorted by three soldiers into the woods: two adults and two children. She wondered whether they had been heading to Saint Girons, towards one of the escape routes over the Pyrenees. Had they been seeking escape and freedom from the Occupiers?

29

Valérie

Saint Girons, France

Claude had warned them again to be alert as they alighted from the train. Lucille was aware of the large number of Gestapo huddled around in groups of two and three on both platforms. All had weapons on display, like badges of honour, she thought. They had the station under constant surveillance. Again Lucille left a train station – this time in a different country and with a different purpose.

Outside the station, Claude gave Jean Paul and Lucille directions to their separate meeting points. Lucille hugged her fellow trainee and bid him au revoir and 'bon chance.' She had grown to respect Colin Russell for his quiet fortitude. She didn't trust herself not to cry as they went their separate ways to who knew what destiny. Claude told her he would see her again of the following day as she walked away from them. She felt an acute sense of isolation: she was now alone in a foreign country and heading to a rendezvous with an unknown agent.

Eventually Lucille located the café meeting point on the corner of the main square and sat at a side table for two in the shade. The day was unseasonably warm. She hid the battered suitcase from prying eyes under the table and crossed her legs in front of it. From here she could observe everyone: the comings and goings of the local people and the enemy's soldiers. The baker's shop next door was closing up. Today's limited bread supplies all sold. The baker gave her a nod as he passed. She wondered whether he was the person she was due to meet. As he put the door key into his trouser pocket, he walked away from his shop.

Five minutes later, a wiry young man slowed his squeaky bicycle in front of the café. He stopped, wheeled his transport up the pavement and leaned it against the closed bakery's window. He approached her table and her heart beat loudly in her eardrums.

"Lucille?"

"Oui, Albert Henri?"

"Oui."

He nodded, pulled out the opposite seat and ordered coffee for them both. The steaming black liquid burnt her tongue and throat. A picture of her last cup of tea with Eleanor rushed into her mind. She wondered where her friend had landed and recalled Eleanor's fear of jumping and injuring an ankle or a wrist. She sent a silent prayer to ask for her friend's safety. Wherever she may be.

Albert furtively passed a scrap of paper across the table to Lucille. She memorised the address scribbled on it, closed her eyes, then nodded. He withdrew it under the cover of his palm, then tipped a cigarette from its box. He offered her one. She declined. After lighting it, he placed the expiring match with the scrap of paper into the ashtray. The small flame died as the smoke curled upwards and disappeared. Paper thin grey ash floated across the table in the breeze that carried away the smell of burning.

After taking a deep drag of the cigarette, he instructed her to take his bicycle, giving her directions to the butcher's shop two streets away. There she was to swap it for a lady's bicycle that was propped up outside the shop, after first purchasing some provisions from Monsieur Henri the shop owner.

"Bon chance." Albert headed off across the square.

Lucille finished her coffee, the bitter dregs at the bottom of the cup making her shiver.

She followed his instructions to the shop and entered it. To her surprise, Albert was serving behind the counter. He made an excuse to fetch some meat from the storage and allowed his father to serve her as arranged. She correctly used the code words parapluie and fromage in her conversation with the butcher. From there she went to the address of the safe house. Lucille found the front door key wrapped up in her purchase from the butcher's shop.

After cycling through side streets and avoiding the main square, she propped her bicycle against the wall next to the shabby front door. Lucille juggled the butcher's parcel and the precious suitcase to retrieve the worn brass key. She felt relief flood through her as she let herself into the ground-floor flat, double checking that no one had followed her. Pleasantly surprised at the homeliness of it, she deposited the wafer-thin slices of meat in the tidy kitchenette area. As she'd exchanged her forged food ration coupons for the supplies, she'd noted that the rate of exchange was higher than in England. However, that did not guarantee bigger quantities or better quality provisions: there was a deliberate Nazi policy to buy the best and most nutritious supplies for themselves. Much of France was starving. She had noticed the beggars in the square, lurking in the shadows to avoid being beaten, threatened or arrest by the soldiers.

Lucille wondered who had occupied the home temporarily before her. And where were they now?

Next, she located the false back panel in the wardrobe and eased it forward. Behind it was a recess in the brickwork where she hid the radio transmitter, carefully replacing the panel and the clothing hanging inside it. Lucille noticed the garments, although few, were her size. She could only bring the basic essentials of underwear, documents, a gun and money with her. Once placed in the drawers of the bedside cabinet, she took off her coat and shoes. Lucille lay down on the bed. The last 36 hours had been a whirlwind of many fearful sights, unfamiliar sounds, and a completely different way of living amongst the enemy. She was weary. She needed to rest before her work began. Her dual role of saboteur and subversive would begin tomorrow.

The next morning a gentle tap on the front door awakened her. Her heart raced. She took a deep breath and opened the door just enough to see Claude through the gap. Relief calmed her nerves. Checking that no one had followed him, he stepped inside. The delicious smell of fresh baking pervaded the hallway.

"Petit déjeuner Lucille."

"Merci Claude."

He offered her the paper bag. Lucille realised she was hungry. His thoughtfulness touched her. Inside, she found warm croissants. Lucille made some fresh, strong coffee and handed a cup to Claude. He smiled warmly at her as she told him she would prefer tea.

"What is it with the English and their tea? I'm surprised they do not send you over with some in your suitcase," he laughed.

Wiping crumbs from his mouth, Claude gave her instructions for the coming week. She was to transmit the messages to London each evening from the network leader and follow any of his instructions. She was to meet him in the park, near the water fountain at noon. The rest of the day she was to observe surreptitiously any troop or police movements in the town as she made her way around. And she must always make sure that she was not being followed.

Around teatime Lucille retrieved some warm dark clothing and the radio set from the wardrobe. Practicality was most important if she had to ride around the French countryside at night, so she pulled on a pair of trousers and a threadbare brown knitted jumper. The left sleeve had a patch at the elbow. The radio set wrapped in a blanket and disguised in an old hatbox. Placing the box in the basket, she wheeled the bicycle out of the hallway.

Lucille headed out of town towards the river. Approaching the old boathouse, she gently applied the brakes and slowed down, looking back over her right shoulder. There was no one around. Once inside the peeling red-painted door, she set up the radio set, handling the fragile glass crystals with great care. They were a rare commodity and easily broken. She coded her first message to London, advising that the local group of Resistants needed more ammunition, weapons and food ration coupons. She thought of her colleagues receiving these messages, just as she had only a few months ago. A smile passed across her lips as she wondered whether Celia was listening to this one. Her concentration strained across her brain and her body – it felt as thin and as fragile as a spider's web as she carefully tapped out the letters according to her 'fist' or code.

Quickly and quietly she hid the radio set in an old cupboard in the dilapidated building. Then she got back in the saddle again and pedalled through the rapidly fading light of dusk back toward the apartment. As she turned into the street, two men approached her in Gestapo uniforms. It was too late: she could not turn round, that would look too obvious. They stopped, and she slowed to a halt. One of them held out his hand and demanded her papers.

Two tense minutes later, they returned them to her. With stern faces they warned her that the curfew had just begun and they did not expect to see Mme Durand on the evening streets again.

As the days passed, she settled into her daily routine. Lucille was pleased to have the comfort of it as a distraction. She missed her home and family; it seemed so long since she had been there. Often she would meet Claude and Albert at the café at the corner of the square and was glad of the company. They would take great inward delight in being in public, under the noses of the Occupiers. They looked like a group of French friends meeting for coffee, conversation and the occasional cognac. Even enduring the austerity and restrictions of war, some aspects of the ordinary life of the town's inhabitants continued. It was a contrast that amazed Lucille. She recognised the stubborn spirit of her father in these modest local people.

A few days later Claude and Albert arrived at the café with a small camera in a brown leather case. Albert told them a local Resistance group leader from the next village had asked him to take some discreet pictures, if they could, of any SS men in their town.

"I'm not sure, but I think they are planning either to kidnap or kill one of them who seems to have taken a liking to the young girls in the village... the Nazis have no morals and have overstepped the mark. Three of their young girls are now with child... it is disgraceful and disrespectful behaviour. It makes me weep."

Lucille observed Claude's face: it was like dark thunder clouds gathering, the anger growing within him. The atrocities of this war never failed to shock her.

"How old is young?" whispered Lucille.

"15 and 16, too young to be mothers to bastard children," he growled.

Lucille felt his sorrow and anger at what was becoming of his homeland and his people. The land that her father had loved.

"So let us do what we can to help these poor souls, if revenge is their intention then so be it. It is not our place to judge, God and history will do that to Monsieur Hitler and his Nazi regime when the war is over. Lucille let's take a walk around the square and up to the church while Albert takes some pictures of us. Make it look like we are a couple, perhaps we have just married?"

Lucille looked at him as her intuition spoke to her. It intrigued her, as his tone was more serious than she was sure he had intended.

Outside the old stone church Claude and Lucille posed on the steps together, Claude's arm casually draped around Lucille's shoulder as they laughed. Albert had a small handheld camera and directed their poses.

"Perfect," said Albert, "a newly married couple." And they all laughed.

A week later Lucille opened the front door to urgent knocking to find Claude on the doorstep. He hurried into the hallway as a soldier passed by. She saw the worried look on his face.

"Lucille, we need help tonight please. Another pair of hands to help lay some explosives on a direct route out of town that only the German soldiers may use. The target is to destroy one bridge over the river. One of our operatives has gone missing – we do not know if they have arrested him, but the conditions will be good this evening. Please take the track to the right of the boathouse after your evening message to London. I will meet you along the path, after a kilometre."

"I must send the message first, there have been troop movements nearby but I will come after that," Lucille replied.

Claude nodded his approval. "You are very diligent in your work here, the others have noticed, especially Monsieur Henri the butcher seems to have taken quite a shine to you. It does not impress Albert." He grinned at her. He waited for her reaction.

"Oh dear, I have not encouraged him, I can assure you!" Lucille was sure she saw a look of relief glance across Claude's face. "After all, I am Madame Durand, a respectable widow, still mourning the sad death of my beloved husband."

Claude noticed a shadow of sadness pass over her usual sunny disposition and wondered what had caused it.

"And are you?" he asked.

"Am I what?"

"A widow? There are many young widows now... and it would make sense that you would undertake such dangerous work for your country and mine, if you wished to avenge your husband's death."

The question had caught Lucille off guard. She stalled for some time to think of an answer. She should reveal none of her background and home situation to fellow Resistants, she knew that. Was this a test? She was missing Marianne and Winnie desperately, and the thought of home bought them closer to her. What should she reply?

Lucille went to the kitchenette area and filled the kettle, to busy her hands and her thoughts. Honesty was to be the best policy.

"No, I am not a widow and I'm not a fiancée either," she took a deep breath, "But, I am a single mother, I have a daughter."

Unconsciously, she bent her head and looked at the patterned rug. She felt Claude step closer to her. As she looked up, he reached out and took her hand. The warmth and pleasure of his action took Lucille by surprise. It had been a long time since a man last held her hand.

"Ah, your child causes the sadness in your eyes."

"She brings me great happiness but I miss her Claude... she is the reason I'm here, to help fight this war and bring peace for us all."

She allowed him to hold her close. In that moment, she felt he understood and did not judge her as a mother of an illegitimate child. The child that she had left behind.

The kettle boiled. She stepped away from him and smiled.

"Your bravery astounds me Lucille – I do not think I am as brave as you, I am humbled by what you have done for us."

"Do not be, there are others, other women and mothers like me."

Claude watched her as she prepared coffee for them both, watching her long slender fingers nimbly go about their task. They sipped their drink in a companionable silence. They need not say anything more. He eked out the time in her company for as long as he dared. Claude knew he needed to begin preparations for the evening sabotage.

"Now I must go Lucille, I will see you later. Please stay safe until then." He pecked her on both cheeks as she let him out.

Later, after she had sent her message to London, Lucille continued on along the narrow riverside track. As she cycled along it, the air was damp and still with an earthy smell to it. All she could hear was her own breathing and the turning of her bicycle wheels. Watching for the meeting point, she saw a movement in the bushes as Claude stepped silently from the shadowy darkness.

"We must leave our bicycles here and proceed on foot, hide it in the undergrowth, quickly." He whispered his order. The tenderness of their earlier encounter had vanished. This was serious, cold-blood-ied work.

They safely hid their escape transport in the long grass and she fol-lowed him. They located the thick wooded area on the side of the River Salat. She guessed they were around half a kilometre from the bridge. He gestured for her to follow him as he crept into the trees. In the dark, a man's voice asked for the password.

"Herrison," she heard Claude whisper. She smiled at the password, meaning hedgehog in English. How appropriate as they moved about in the fading light of the day in the undergrowth.

Lucille noticed Albert, and he nodded. He was a man of few words. The friendly baker was standing behind him, together with another woman and a young boy. They all nodded at her. The woman extended her hand to Lucille.

"Bonjour, je suis Céleste."

"Lucille."

Lucille was to assist Claude in attaching the explosives to the bridge structure while Céleste, Albert, and the baker prepared the detonation cables. They separated in different directions, disappearing into the darkness. The skinny young boy, only twelve or thirteen, was their lookout. Claude's eyes had a haunted look as he told her that the authorities had deported the boy's Jewish parents to a labour camp. The baker had adopted him as his own, hiding him in his shop. It amazed Lucille that the boy evaded forced work for the enemy.

As Claude and Lucille reached the bridge, she saw a movement ahead of them, under the next archway. She tapped Claude's shoulder and gestured to the place of the movement. He nodded and gave her the thumbs up sign.

"It is Albert. He will join us in a moment."

Claude attached the explosives to the base of the structure and gestured to Lucille to attach the detonator and timer. She frantically tried to recall the explosives training classes. The lessons she had listened to carefully and the practical exercise in the manor house grounds escaped her for a moment. What if she got the order of the wires the wrong way around? If she cross wired them, then their effort would be for nothing. Her mind went blank. Think, think. What had they taught her? The memory of Frank Lawrence failing this task came to mind. She felt a panic in her stomach and counted to ten to relax. It worked. She remembered the procedure and with faltering hands she attached the detonation equipment. Albert silently appeared beside them. Anxiously, he looked at his watch.

"We must leave now," he urged, "We need the cover of the woods, quickly."

As Claude and Lucille ran ahead, Albert followed. He had secured a tree branch to his waist earlier, and now used it to sweep the path, in order to cover their tracks and footprints in the soft earth. They made their way back along the riverside to the woods. Breathless, they crouched down in the dewy grass as they waited. Albert discarded the branch.

It felt like an eternity. Lucille's nerves were like shards of shattered glass being walked upon. She could almost hear the crunching sound in her head. Her awareness of every sound, movement and smell in the air was painful.

Suddenly an ear-splitting explosion made her flinch and cover her ears as the night sky erupted into red and yellow flames. The noise reverberated around the valley as the silhouetted outline of timbers, twisted metalwork and black smoke arose like a spectre from the inferno. The debris leapt into the sky against the blaze, then fell into the water below. Lucille made out the miniature shapes of people and vehicles plunging into the depths below. In the distance they appeared to be the size of toy soldiers being tossed away by a spoilt child. An acrid, smoky, charred smell hung in the air.

Claude grabbed Lucille's hand and pulled her up from the undergrowth. He flung her bicycle into the path.

"Go fast, now," he ordered and turned away to pull his and Albert's bicycles from their hiding place.

If the Germans had looked closely with binoculars, they would have seen three tiny figures on bicycles pedalling as fast as they could along the riverside away from the bridge. Away from the scene of death, devastation and sabotage that they had caused.

30

Valérie

Two days later

Lucille was returning to the apartment after a daylight afternoon transmission of a message to London, confirming the sabotage of the bridge had been successful. However, the consequences of their destruction were a 5pm curfew on the residents of the small town. She could not risk being out after this to send her messages. She decided it was safer to continue to conceal the radio set at the old boathouse for at least another day. She would look for a new location for it tomorrow. Her meagre rations of food occupied her thoughts as she crossed the town square. Hurrying and pulling her headscarf tight around her dark curls, she heard the heavy military trucks drive into the space. Concealing herself and her bicycle in an alley, she carefully poked her head around the corner of the stone building.

What she saw turned her stomach. Only by being conscious of her breathing could she control the urge to be sick. The biliousness rose from the pit of her empty stomach. She watched as the Nazi soldiers flung open the back doors of one of three field trucks, then roughly drag two people from it. Soldiers with rifles and dogs poured from the other two vehicles and filled the square with their ominous presence. The shouting, the snarling dogs and the sheer number of oppressor uniforms silenced the passers-by. The fading sunlight of the evening cast long shadows across the cobbles of the square. She recognised the handcuffed, chained and bloodied young woman sprawled on the floor.

"Céleste," she gasped. Then she realised that the other body was Albert. She clamped her hand tightly over her mouth to stop herself shouting their names.

The senior ranking officer barked orders at the onlookers to stand still, they were not to leave the square. No one dared move. Their fear hung in the air, still and unseen. Then he shouted at the prisoners to kneel on the stone cobbles.

Then there was an eerie silence Lucille found deafening inside her head. The implications of her fellow Resistants arrest were too big to fit inside her brain. She could not think straight. Her legs shook uncontrollably. The officer turned to his men and pointed at two of them: with rigid obedience they stepped forward and positioned themselves behind the handcuffed and chained figures. The uniformed men raised their rifles. The officer raised his hand and as he lowered it, each fired one shot into the back of their captive's heads.

The brutality of the act jolted her from inertia. Lucille snatched her bicycle from the wall. She knew in her heart that she was in terrible danger. She dared not look back. The frozen picture of the two corpses ingrained into her vision: limp bodies on the hard ground, discarded human beings that looked like rag dolls. They reminded her of Marianne's rag doll, Sammy. The thought consumed her. Her fear and anger urged her on to pedal with all her strength through the back streets in a random direction. They must not follow me. She chanted the mantra in her mind. Now she knew with her whole being that she had made the right decision to accept this work, to play her part in defeating such tyranny and cruelty.

Lucille reached the apartment and collapsed on to the bed. Her hunger had evaporated. Was she safe here? Should she leave now? But where would she go? The priority was to think calmly, rationally. She did not know who she could trust. They had tortured their captives. Of that there was no doubt. What if they had confessed and given the Occupiers the details of the other perpetrators? Had they betrayed the rest of the local organisation? Would they come for her next? If they arrested her, she could not claim to be British nor claim prisoner of war status. She held French papers. And false ones at that.

In the half light, she could hear people scurrying around outside. A sound interrupted her racing thoughts. A gentle tapping on the back kitchenette window. She opened the internal wooden shutter slightly and saw Claude lurking in the shadow. He deftly climbed in through the window.

"We are in danger, we must leave immediately... I will return in 10 minutes, sooner if we can avoid the roadblocks they are setting up. They know it takes several people to destroy a bridge."

"Have they arrested Monsieur Henri? What about the Jewish boy? Where will we go to? And what about the radio transmitter? I must fetch it."

"No, they are still in the shop, but he serves a purpose for the Germans, providing food. Anyway, there is no time, and it is too dangerous to fetch the radio... there are other duties you can help us with... we need people to... I will tell you later. We will get a message to London somehow... now hurry, I'll return quickly.."

He stared at Lucille's pale and shocked face, kissed her quickly on her cheek and then disappeared through the window.

She put on another layer of clothes and then wrapped yesterday's bread and a piece of cheese in a small towel. She stuffed the provisions in her coat pocket. The tap on the front window made her jump. As she opened the door, she checked her coat pocket contents. Claude seized her hand, and all but threw her in the back of Monsieur Henri's van. He jumped inside after her. As the butcher pulled away, they concealed themselves under crates and sacks. There was an imperceptible smell of blood.

31

Valérie

The foothills of the Pyrenees

Lucille did not know where they were going, only that she was glad to have Claude by her side. She took some deep breaths to steady her shaking hands and thoughts as the truck threw them about. How would she get a message to London to tell them of the turn of events? No one knew where she was. She was afraid. She cried and as she did Claude found her hand and held it again. His warm fingers held hers and she was thankful to be with him. Lucille tried to distract her fear by thinking of Marianne and Winnie. What were they doing at home at this moment?

They had tried to sleep huddled and concealed in the back of Monsieur Henri's van. Lucille had propped herself up against Claude's shoulder. It had proved to be a fitful and fruitless exercise, partly because of the constant jolting as they travelled along country lanes and partly because of the pervading smell of meat and blood in the sawdust in the cracks and crannies of the vehicle. She felt cold. It was the shock reaction to the events in the square.

Claude sensed that in her quietness she felt troubled and afraid. He knew she was sure, yet also unsure of her reasons for being here now. Her bravery and willingness to put herself in danger had impressed him. Little did she know she was about to take on another life-threatening task to help those fleeing persecution.

After several hours, the van stopped at their rendezvous point. Lucille heard the silence of the countryside. Monsieur Henri opened the doors, and she saw an abandoned barn. Claude climbed down from the vehicle. They helped Lucille down and they all stretched their legs. They waited side by side in the first light of the new morning.

"What are we waiting for?" Lucille whispered.

"Our fellow fighters for the cause," Claude replied.

"I must leave now to avoid any suspicion, stay safe and travel well my compatriots. We will avenge my son's murder," Monsieur Henri said. Then he hugged them both close.

As the sound of the engine faded, they crept into the barn and hid behind some old bales of hay.

"I did not realise that Albert was Monsieur Henri's son... his heart breaks," Lucille whispered. "Surely all this suffering and violence isn't in vain Claude? It must bring freedom and peace for our children and their children." Her angry whisper shook him from his thoughts of what lay ahead.

Lucille looked at Claude and he saw a memory of Marianne haunted her tired eyes. Her heartache was raw, etched on her face as she frowned.

"Freedom and peace will indeed overcome tyranny in the end... they must."

The faint crunch of gravel disturbed the silence outside. Approaching footsteps. The door creaked open. Someone made a tapping noise on the ground with a metal implement. Claude placed his index finger to his lips and bid her silence. Then the tapping noise repeated. Claude gave a soft whistle in response. The unseen person repeated the tapping on the ground. He motioned to Lucille. They stepped into view of their compatriots. A determined looking young man accompanied a young woman through the door. He was a double, a replica of her, her twin brother. Claude recognised them from his last meeting there. Manuel and Elena - their Spanish counterparts. At their feet was a thin sandy dog with inquisitive eyes.

"Ah Claude, we are happy to see you again," said Elena quietly. She shook his hand and kissed both of his cheeks.

"I did not expect to be back so soon, but we must move Lucille out of danger, back to London if it is at all possible."

"Welcome friends, we shall do what we can," said Manuel.

Lucille and Claude told them about the events of the last few days in St. Girons: the successful sabotage and extensive damage to the bridge and the executions in the market square. They did not know whether their operations had now compromised their network. And he needed a wireless operator from their network with the codes to contact London to send a message about her urgent withdrawal from the town. He also had a request for more support with weapons, ammunition, money and general supplies. Elena and Manuel glanced at each other and nodded gravely. Claude impressed on them he thought that it too dangerous for Lucille to remain there.

"Both sides will win and lose in this war. There are many ways to do both," said Manuel.

"Lucille, we are happy that you are here with us now, we are grateful for your help and the help from the British Government in our work." Elena touched her arm, speaking with sincerity.

Manuel was more dismissive, "Some of our countrymen think that Mr Churchill is arrogant and foolish taking on the Nazis and dragging us all into this war."

Lucille nodded but remained silent. She had not been aware that other countries viewed the UK, and its Governments decisions in this way.

"Now Manuel, politics of countries will not make Europe free again, be quiet. We must leave here and go to the safe house, we need to rest and prepare before we start on our next escort trip." Elena threw him a dark look.

Lucille recognised Elena's attempt to ease the tension of her brother's comments to their new acquaintance and was grateful. It reminded her of her father's ability to pour oil on troubled waters.

"Where are we going? What am I going to help you with?"

"I know you're aware of the escape lines Lucille... we think it is best if you assist a group of people on the next crossing of the Pyrenees... help them and yourself to escape to Spain... then on to freedom."

Lucille gave Claude a look of astonishment. Her dark eyes glanced around the group.

"I'm aware of the organisation of the escape lines yes, but I'm not trained in these activities Claude, and we don't seem to have any equipment… surely I would be more useful to you here delivering messages to London about the Germans activity and…"

"Lucille, you are more useful alive, whether you are here or in England. By making the crossing they can hide you in Spain for a short time while we make the arrangements for you to return home, possibly via Gibraltar… I'm sure the English authorities will be glad to see you and to send you back into France again. You can then return to help us."

"There must be another way, surely? Could I head for the coast and find a troop ship or a boat to get me back to England?"

Claude shook his head. She trusted he was telling the truth.

"And what if I say I won't go with you to Spain?" she challenged him. She felt they were deciding for her and she was losing control of her own choices.

Manuel was blunt as he gruffly said, "Listen! Listen to me - you do not have a choice, you have run out of options… you are not safe in France. The Gestapo and the SS will have your name and be hunting for you now. If they catch you and identify that you were part of the group for the bridge sabotage, then… well… I doubt they will allow you to live. You are here illegally and no one from England can help you now."

Claude sighed. Lucille understood the inevitability of her position and the path she must now follow. Claude took her hand and pulled her close to him.

"Manuel is correct, you - and I – we do not have a choice. If we wish to avoid arrest my brave friend, then there is no alternative…

we will not see our longed for peace and freedom if we do not escape now. There are many ways to fight a battle. Sometimes knowing when to retreat is an excellent tactic. And for you - you must think of Marianne's future."

"Oh Claude, I would rather stay here and help you all but I know you are right."

"I will be part of this crossing, as I too am a wanted man, Lucille."

The mention of Marianne hammered home the enormity of the effort she must make to see her again. The journey to reach safety and ultimately England relied on these Resistants, strangers and their efforts on her behalf. She must rely on them and their contacts along the way. She was in their hands and at their mercy. While the thought of crossing high mountains terrified her, she felt a calm resignation and an acceptance of her fate. She must gracefully accept their help and the risks they were taking for her to reach the sanctuary of her home again.

"I see, then I have to go with you. What do I have to do to help you? When do we leave?"

SAINT-GIRONS

REFUGE DES ESTAGNOUS

FRANCE

SPAIN

P Y R E N E E S

ALOS D'ISIL

ESTERRI d'ANEU

32

Valérie

The crossing

It was dark now. The bedraggled, frozen group trudged on, heads bowed and each with their own thoughts. There was a silvery darkness when the moon slipped behind the clouds. Lucille guessed it was the early hours of the morning, around 2 o'clock. They had been walking uphill for an exhausting, leg sapping four hours. The wind was picking up: a lazy wind, the kind that cut right through you instead of going round you. She hoped that there wouldn't be a fresh snowfall as she grimaced: she'd grazed her ankle against the rocks, trying to make out the path in front of her, as much of a path as it was. She stepped forward carefully, the dim torch flickering as she placed her icy hands on the rocks and felt the way forward. The thin gloves gave no warmth, and even if they had been any thicker, she could not have manoeuvred her hands over the jagged outcrops of the Pyrenees, anyway.

She knew her limbs could feel every little intrusion – the icy wind whipping her thin layered clothing against her arms and legs, the inadequate wet boots that had frozen, now welded to her feet and the knitted hat kept very little heat that was useful. The wind howled in her ears: she hoped that the painful numbness in her left lobe wasn't the start of frostbite.

Her body ached with cold, hunger, and fatigue: her wasted muscles were hugging her bones as best they could, and yet her body felt heavy. But she must keep going, guiding these strangers across the mountains of the French border with Spain. Like her, the Spanish siblings would hand the unlikely group of travellers to other Resistance workers, who would help them escape from the Nazis.

As she followed the group, Claude trudged on ahead of her. There was something about him that reminded her of her father. Perhaps it was the pride and dignity of the French? In the darkness she bowed under the burden of their responsibility: their task of delivering the Austrian Jewish family plus an American and a British pilot weighed heavily on their shoulders. She wondered whether their journey would be successful in these conditions. Would the family find a refuge from persecution for their faith? Would they ever be free to worship under their old beliefs again?

Claude suggested a brief rest stop. Thankfully, Manuel agreed. Lucille hunkered down against the rocks facing out of the wind and motioned for the family to do the same. Retrieving the dwindling rations of food from her backpack, she shared around the stale bread and dry cheese.

"Here, take some of my bread Ma'am." The weary American offered her half of his small amount of bread.

He had watched with admiration as she gave her portion to the young Jewish boy crouching next to her. Lucille nodded her head. They kept communication to a minimum. The darkness lifted as the moon returned from its journey behind the clouds.

"How much further do we have to walk, Mama?" the boy whispered.

The mother looked at Lucille, her dark-circled, frightened eyes appealing for some help and reassurance.

Lucille quietly assured the boy and hugged him close, "When the sun rises again you will be in a new country and you will be free." She felt the tears of this frightened boy as he allowed a stranger to hold him. His mother gave her a gracious nod of thanks, recognising in Lucille her similar longing for assurance that Marianne was safe and well. She could not help the thoughts that rushed into her mind: men might die in war through armed combat, but women sacrificed their lives and their hearts too.

Manuel and Elena raised their forefingers to their lips to remind the family and the pilots that they required silence at all times while they were on the move. The young boy stood up, approached the little dog and slipped on the ice.

"Ouch! Mama!" he cried out.

Manuel's thunderous look at the boy's mother and father frightened them, "Shhh! You will put us in danger." His whisper was fierce.

The boy's mother helped him up. Lucille could see that he had injured his wrist or his fingers, his face scored with pain. He cried more silent tears and cradled his hand to his chest. The Spaniards' little dog went and sat next to the boy and nuzzled his side. The boy gave a painful sob and stroked the animal's head.

After half an hour, the exhausted party clambered slowly over the rocks and climbed higher through the last mountain pass. The little dog led the way through the harsh landscape, as though following the scent trail of home.

The stiff wind continued to swirl around them: it howled like an unseen but watching animal. Lucille watched the thin Jewish family struggle to keep pace. The father's body bowed against the elements as he struggled to protect his baby daughter. After another hour of slow progress, she tapped his shoulder and made signs to take his baby daughter from him. He tenderly handed her over, straightened his back and bowed his head deeply in thanks to her. The tiny body slept snuggly as she placed it under her coat, against her body. Lucille was thankful for the warmth that the little bundle gave her. Thoughts of Marianne crept into the cold numbness in her head. What was Marianne doing now? Was she safe? Was she happy?

The early pink light of the dawn deepened and crept across the clear sky. The wind retreated.

"This Col is the highest point of the crossing, we approach the border. There is Spain. Welcome." Manuel proudly swept his arms wide. Even the dog stopped and looked across the dimly lit mountain vista, as though it knew it was coming home.

As they descended from the thin air and the altitude of the mountains, Lucille was glad to be leaving the prominent ridges and snow line. The new day had dawned. Manuel had given them instructions that they must take extra care, be alert to any sounds. Elena had told her they knew that Spanish collaborators and some enemy patrols intermittently waited in the mountains for escapers and evaders. The enemy trained them to listen for sounds and movement in this uninhabited place. The collaborators were prepared to report those fleeing persecution and death, in exchange for extra food and protection. They hid out in the lower plateaus of the mountains. The scruffy little brown terrier kept going at the head of the party. His paws skipped the rocks and following an unseen route. He wagged his tail.

The sun was a growing yellow ball, casting feint shadows through the fingers of clouds in the mountains. There was a tangible feeling of relief among them: the weary party was now out of the wind and snow. The slight warmth was more than welcome on their faces and their bodies after the bitter coldness of the night.

Freedom in a new day beckoned them forward. They had experienced the worst of their trek as pine trees and vegetation rose to meet their wet feet. They descended the steep sides of another valley.

They rested briefly after another hour. Lucille thought of Marianne again as she handed the tiny baby girl back to her father. She felt the child's warmth evaporate from her body. Her quandary deepened: would she return home to the comfort and warmth of her home with Marianne and Winnie? One thing was for sure was that despite the air raids, they were relatively safe there. Or did she remain in enemy territory for a while longer and channel her efforts into helping the French Resistance?

Lucille handed around the last pieces of bread, again forgoing hers for the family. Sitting next to Claude, their backs against a tree, she closed her eyes. But she knew she must not sleep, despite the fatigue in her muscles. She felt Claude gently take her hand and kiss her on the cheek.

Back on their feet again, the group pressed on and made the continued descent of a hillside. Her spirits rose as they saw the sparkling water of the River Pallaresa meandering through the valley below them. Elena told her that their destination was the village of Alos d'Isil, where they were to deliver their so-called 'packets' – the human cargo they were escorting to freedom.

Slowly and steadily the weary party kept going, one foot in front of another. They could do little else. By lunchtime they reached the outskirts of the village, and Manuel halted the group.

"Quickly, we must disperse, you are not yet safe and no one must see us," he said.

Hurriedly each exchanged a thank you and a goodbye. The Jewish family, the Americans and Lucille and Claude shared a deep sense of relief. Manuel and Elena would ensure that they delivered their consignment to the next helpers on the journey to freedom. Lucille did not trust herself to speak as the tears in her eyes and the constriction in her throat threatened to break free. She hugged them all and then turned to the Jewish mother. There was a deep connection with this stranger as she held her in her arms. This woman who had experienced the terror and fear of the war on a different scale to her. Yet Lucille felt it united them in their determination to overcome life-threatening tyranny, to keep their children safe and give them freedom.

The family, the pilots, and Elena disappeared into the back of a local baker's waiting for them across the road. It trundled into the distance, whipping up the dust as they headed on their next leg of the journey to freedom. Exhausted, Lucille stood with Manuel and Claude.

"Come, we must walk a little further to get indoors, you must hide, they will notice a stranger Lucille – although I think you will blend in well, you have the dark Spanish looks."

Her heart sank. She didn't think that she could move her legs and feet any further forward. She glanced down and realised that her ankle was bleeding where she had caught it on the boulder.

"It's not far, if I remember correctly," Claude encouraged her.

"You have been here before?" she quizzed him.

"Yes, once... I have assisted the escape line before. A group of educated young Jewish people – an engineer, a scientist and a lawyer from Vienna - their parents paid for false papers for them to leave. We will base the peace of the future in knowledge and education so that we do not find ourselves in this situation again. And our young people are that future."

"Let us pray we don't have to endure this again Claude – nor our children."

After twenty minutes walking out of Alos d'Isil, they reached a dilapidated red roofed cottage set a few hundred metres back off the road. The rear door creaked as they entered. Flakes of blue paint fell from it to the floor.

"Rest here for today. Use only this room and the room next door, not the rooms at the front of the house - do not arouse any suspicion that anyone is here," order Manuel.

Lucille looked around the sparse kitchen with an old wooden table, two chairs and a cupboard. It amazed her that the furniture was there and not used for firewood.

"You will find a tap outside for water and some food in the cupboard that my Aunt has left for you. I will return tomorrow with some news of your route home... if I can find the radio operator tonight. He will send a message to London for us."

"Thank you." Claude shook Manuel's hand.

"Yes, thank you Manuel – and thank you to Elena too. I am grateful to you both for getting me out of France."

"Now I must leave – you have weapons don't you?"

"Yes," chorused Claude and Lucille, both too tired to say anything else.

Lucille picked up a jug from the shelf and followed Manuel out of the door. When she returned with water, she saw Claude had sliced some bread and placed it with some meat on plates.

"I must wash this ankle first." She went into the adjoining room and noted the two single beds. Neatly folded clean clothes were on a chair in between them. She poured some water into the bowl on the primitive washstand, undressed and washed. There wasn't any soap, but there was a threadbare washcloth. Lucille thought that never had a wash felt so luxurious. She dried herself on the discarded shirt and sorted through the clean clothes that were all men's. She dressed in a shirt and pair of trousers, then pulled a jumper on top.

When she re-entered the small kitchen room, she saw Claude with his head on his left arm on the table. His pistol lay beside his right hand. A snore escaped from his mouth. Lucille touched his shoulder and in one fluid action he jumped up with the firearm in his hand.

"Don't shoot Claude! It's me."

"Oh! Lucille, you made me jump, I apologise." It horrified him to see the gun in his hand pointing at her.

"We are tired, and in a strange place - it is a natural reaction, don't worry. Put it down," she said.

"Your foot, is it ok?"

"It has a deep cut, but it will heal if I can keep it dry. Now let's eat." Lucille pulled out the kitchen chair, it scraped loudly across the stone floor and echoed around the room. She froze as they glanced at each other, aware that it was too much noise. Had they dropped their guard so soon? Lucille picked up the chair and then sat down. The relief of relative safety flooded through her.

"And I found this in the cupboard," said Claude triumphantly, holding a bottle of wine. Dislodging the cork stopper with his pocket knife, he poured the red liquid into two earthenware cups.

"What I wouldn't give for some cold lemonade, Claude, but we'll have to make do with wine instead."

After their meal they sat with the silence and the wine, neither wanting to voice their thoughts. To do so might shatter the fragile moment, and they knew they could not put it together again.

"What will you do now Claude?"

"I will return over the mountains to France, but by a different route and continue my work there." He trailed off with a sadness in his voice that spoke to her.

"When will you return?"

"I expect I will leave in a day or two..."

"Ah, I see, so soon... Claude I must tell you this – er, I have decided that I don't want to return to England, not yet anyway. I'll hide here and then return to France with you. I decided when we crossed the

Spanish border I could not abandon this vital work and go home yet. The fight for freedom isn't over, and there is growing hope of victory in Europe. I've heard of a proposed Allied invasion. We must not give up yet. I cannot give up yet, Claude."

"But you have to go back home... you are a wanted person by the German authorities... and in hiding you the others are taking substantial risks and are in grave danger. You cannot think just of yourself, Lucille, and you do not need me to remind you... there is little Marianne to think of."

His voice was stern, and the concerned look on his face caught Lucille by surprise. She knew if she stayed she could spend a little more precious time with Claude, but that was not the principal reason behind her decision. Had she misinterpreted their moments of tenderness over recent weeks? Surely not.

"Don't you think I'm not aware of that every day? I know she will miss me – but I feel I have to stay a while longer and help some more. If it is too difficult to be in France, then I could help Manuel and Elena with the mountain crossings to freedom... I have made my decision."

"So be it, let us discuss this with Manuel tomorrow, before he goes any further in finding a safe passage for you. Now we should sleep, I think."

33

Marianne

Childhood memories - November 1947

I drifted in and out of a shallow sleep for a while. In the twilight between waking and slumber, I recalled another memory. I was a few years older now, a feeling of the weight of more responsibility came back to me.

"The post has been grandma."

I had picked up the letter from the mat at the front door as I hung my coat up on the bannister at the bottom of the stairs. As usual, I sat on the bottom step, unbuckling my black scuffed school shoes. I was going to be in trouble with her for running around in the playground: decent shoes were still scarce, she said, I must look after them.

Grandma was drying her hands as she turned around from the sink. She was in her usual place; it seemed to me. I placed the letter on the kitchen table as she went to the pantry. I did not recognise the handwriting. She returned with our usual tea of bread and thin red jam.

"What did you learn at school today, then?"

"Oh... just the usual things like spellings and sums and something about the Romans."

"What's the matter, Marianne? You're quiet, cat got your tongue? Let me look at you... have you been crying?"

I tried to evade grandmas scrutiny of my face but it was a useless task: she always seemed to know when I was feeling sad. I concluded it must be a magic power that grandmothers possessed.

"It's nothing, Grandma."

I set about fetching some plates from the cupboard and laying the table for tea to avoid her gaze.

"I think it is something Marianne, now please tell me - what or who has upset you?"

There was going to be no escape from this interrogation, I could tell. We wouldn't be having tea until I told her.

"Well... just some girls were calling me names in the playground, that's all... but I said what you told me to say about them being really lucky to have a mum and a dad at home. And that I'm special because I have you at home. And then they left me alone, so that's alright now."

"And was Dorothy one of these children? She's supposed to be your friend, I'll be speaking to her mother when I see her, if she is saying cruel things to you."

"No Grandma, she isn't saying the things, she was just showing off her new shoes. I think that she's frightened not to be in that group... so that they don't say nasty things about her... oh Grandma, why do they have to be like that and make me cry? I'm a girl like them and I do all my lessons... sometimes I think it's because I can speak some French like my mum and grandpa Phillipe could and they can't."

"Oh Marianne, come here."

I dutifully did as I was bid. Grandma gave me one of her cuddles that always made me feel better. It was the smell of the yellow tar soap that always reminded me of home.

"Now, I don't like people, and especially children who brag about things, so you just ignore her. When we have enough coupons saved up, we'll get you a new one. And promise me Marianne that you will tell your teacher if they hurt you at all. And you carry on being you – you're just as good as them and know lots of things about the world that they don't."

Her reassuring voice and constant comfort wrapped me up in love in our kitchen.

"Let me cut the bread for you Grandma while you open the letter."

I had already taken the bread knife from the drawer and unwrapped the white loaf. As I cut thin slices of bread, silence invaded the room. I had felt this silence somewhere before. It felt familiar and was so loud in my ears that it screamed a warning sound that something had shifted, a sign of change. Grandma sat down heavily in the kitchen chair, staring at the letter in her hand. Her left hand placed a photograph of two people on the table. It was a man and a woman. And when she turned it over, I could see some writing on the back of it, but I couldn't read it.

"Grandma?"

She did not answer. She looked up and towards the window, as though someone was standing there. But there wasn't anyone there.

"What is it, Grandma?"

I knew I had felt this icy fear before too, familiar like an emptiness, a space that refuses to fill.

"Oh, Marianne... will we ever stop missing her?"

A tear, like a raindrop, trickled down her cheek. She silently and gently put the letter and photograph in the pocket of her faded pinafore.

I never asked about the photograph as I did not want to make her sad again. Still believing that it was my job to keep grandma alive and that I could not, outwardly at any rate, be too sad. I couldn't let her see my grief and loss, so that she wouldn't die of a broken heart. Yet somehow I knew it was a photograph of Maman. Who had sent it? And why?

"You've got me though, Grandma."

I placed the knife on the plate and went around the table to hug her. Somehow I knew it was the right thing to do, even as young as I was. I felt as if I grew up that day, that the burden of caring for her had been silently, invisibly passed into my hands and the weight of it placed on my shoulders. Grandma needed me to be strong and I couldn't help but think that, just perhaps, mum would have wanted me to be so too.

This memory felt new to me, or if not new, then one that hadn't seen the light of day for over fifty years. I had spent most of the night searching the past for clues - and I had found nothing new to help me there. I trusted that as I arose, the future would reveal the truth to me.

34

Marianne

Meeting Jacques

After waking with a fuzzy headed hangover from the previous evening's Martinis, I showered and pulled myself together. A breakfast of croissants, jam and coffee did the trick.

"Are you sure you want to do this?" asked Janet as we left our hotel room key at the reception desk.

"Yes, I'm sure. We'll see if we can talk to Jacques. If I don't go now, I'm sure I'll change my mind."

An hour later I pulled up in front of the red front door of number 27. The only sound in the narrow, quiet country lane was a family of sparrows twittering and squabbling, as they do the world over.

I knocked at the front door and waited. I hadn't known before, but I'd gone through a lifetime of waiting for this moment. The immaculately kept exterior was welcoming, yet the front door remained resolutely in place: there were no sounds of movement inside. I knocked again, louder this time.

"Typical, looks like we're out of luck today, just when I'd built up the courage!"

"Perhaps not Marianne, the café owner's mother has just been watching us from her window... listen, she's unlocking her front door."

An elderly lady with a pinafore tentatively opened the door. "Bonjour, Monsieur Allard est parti un jour."

"Maman, the ladies are English," said the café owner behind her, "She said that her neighbour, the man you wish to speak to, is away today."

"Ah, thank you. I'm sorry to trouble you, but does your Maman know what time he will be back?"

The elderly lady looked at her son as he translated. She nodded, and he replied, "Mr Allard has gone to visit his daughter in Perpignan, he will return tomorrow morning. Maman said she will tell him you have called."

"Thank you, we shall visit again tomorrow then."

The relief of not having to face whatever was coming filled me. But it was fleeting. As we spent some time touring about the region and the day wore on in to evening, I knew I would have another sleepless night. I was so close to meeting Jacques Allard and yet so far away.

The next morning I felt nervous. This was the day, then? After agonising over what to wear I decided on a navy linen shift dress with a colourful scarf: Janet approved of it as a casual yet chic look of not-being-black-in-mourning and with-a-touch-of-tasteful-colour. She drove the now familiar route to the village. My nerves were too on edge to concentrate. As the scenery passed by, I practised the questions in my head. The ones I would ask Jacques.

"Do you think we should have called first? Just showing up on his doorstep like this might be a bit of a shock for him."

"We're here now, and anyway I'm sure the neighbour will have told him we were here yesterday."

We parked in the quiet country lane again, and I knocked on the door, again. When it opened, a woman beamed at me.

"Marianne, hello, welcome, and your friend. Grand-père is expecting you. Please come in and I'll call him, he's out in the garden somewhere." She stepped back and invited us into the hallway.

"Let me take you through and I'll make you both a drink. I'm Amelie by the way."

We followed her into a cosy pale blue living room at the back of the house, looking out on to a magnificent garden with colourful flower borders. Through the open doors, the man from the funeral was pushing a wheelbarrow up the path towards the house. We stepped out onto a delightful patio area.

The squeaking wheelbarrow ground to a halt. He removed his gardening gloves and placed them on top of the weeds and grass cuttings. And there stood Jacques Allard, more stooped than I recalled from our first brief meeting. He smiled.

"Bonjour Monsieur Allard, I'm sorry to call on you without ringing first, I hope you don't mind. This is my best friend Janet."

"Aah, Marianne, yes I know. I have been waiting for you, my dear." Stepping towards me, he kissed me on both cheeks, then held my arms gently and looked at me. It was as though he was in a faraway place of memories. His voice was almost a whisper.

"You are so much like her." His voice croaked. He cleared his throat and repeated the same warm gesture with Janet. When he moved away, I was unsure whether Jacques had the watery eyes of an elderly man or they were tears threatening to brim over onto his cheeks.

"I think that you have been resourceful to find me here." I wasn't sure whether this was an accusation or a question. Perhaps he had not wanted a reminder of the war or the past to find him.

"Please forgive me if I'm interrupting you, I can come back another day... I'm sorry to contact you out of the blue like this... I wrote to your previous address, so I'm guessing that you have not received the letter."

"No, no, please stay, you are welcome. Yes, I have eventually received your letter. The new owners of my other house brought your letter to me last week. And then another coincidence: my new neighbour's son told me you were here, in France, looking for me. I was very surprised. And I was very much looking forward to seeing you. I am pleased to see you again. It is an honour to have you and your friend here... well, well, Valérie's daughter, after all these years... I have not expected this in my lifetime."

At the mention of my mum I felt fragile and raw, yet a peculiar fresh energy also arose in me. So here I was with a tangible connection to my childhood past. I wondered whether I was a link to a past he preferred to forget.

"And how have you been keeping since Winnie's passing? Please take a seat."

The gentle voice sounded genuinely concerned for my welfare. His enquiry touched me.

"I'm well, thank you for asking Mr Allard."

I hoped he couldn't tell that this was a white lie, that he hadn't guessed that I had spent several days wallowing in my grief and desolation. Did I want or need this stranger to think well of me? He seemed to think highly of grandma and mum.

"Marianne, I understand... this is a sad time for you."

"Thank you, Mr Allard. Er... I think we need to talk, if you don't mind... there are some things I need to ask you about... my mother."

"Yes, of course you do... and please call me Jacques. I have things I need to tell you too."

"Oh... do you?"

Amelie breezed through the open kitchen door with a tray of glasses and a jug.

"Right Grand-père, sit yourself down and take a rest, you've done enough for one day, I think. I've made fresh lemonade, I hope you like lemonade Marianne, if not I can make you something else."

"No, that's wonderful, thank you Amelie. Lemonade is my favourite." I hadn't realised that I was thirsty after the journey.

"And we hope that you'll stay for lunch with us. I thought a late lunch around 3 o'clock would be nice... so that you'll have lots of time to talk and enjoy this sunshine we're having. Is that ok for you?"

"Amelie, thank you, but only if it's not too much trouble," I said.

"We insist, don't we Grand-père?"

"Yes, my darling girl, that's fine, what would I do without you?" He blew her a theatrical kiss as she walked away.

"Well, now." He said no more. He sipped his drink. "I'd much prefer a Martini, but my granddaughter doesn't approve of me having an apéritif so early in the day. At my age it can't really do me any harm, I'm sure. After all, I survived the war."

We sat on opposite sides of the outdoor table, enjoying the summer warmth on our faces. We enjoyed a few moments of comfortable silence. I sensed that both of us wanted to say the right thing. I was still unsure whether I was ready for what the forthcoming time would reveal.

"Jacques... I don't know where to begin to be honest... I have so many questions."

"I'm sure you do, and I will do my best to answer them for you."

"First, how on earth did you know my grandmother had died if you live here?"

"My grandson left France to work in England five or six years ago. Matthew lives in Newbury now, near to you, and he saw your announcement in the local paper. He recognised the surname Bouchard and remembered that I had spoken of it when he was younger. He thought it might interest me, so he called me up. And I recognised your grandmother's name immediately."

"I suppose it is an unusual last name in the UK."

"I had to come and pay my respects Marianne; I do hope that I did not offend you."

"Thank you for coming, I appreciate it was a lot of travelling for you. It did not offend me, quite the opposite, I was intrigued about you said... that you knew my mum during the war. What did you mean, Jacques?"

Jacques was gazing at me, but not seeing me. I knew I had intruded on his private thoughts.

"Ah, yes... the brave and lovely Valérie... Marianne, the things I know... some of them are difficult and I have told no one of them before today... I have saved them in my heart. But now it is time for you to know the truth."

I thought I had held the truth, but the events of the last few weeks were pulling my beliefs about my mother out of my hands. It appeared they were in a different place, in an alternative reality. A place that was somewhere in the past and in a world different to the one I knew.

"So were you stationed in England during the war? Is that how you met her?"

"We met in the autumn of 1943... but no, not in England... it was here, in France."

Now I knew for certain this was the Claude in the photograph. And it was a relief.

"I did not know that she had been in France during the war, and grandma never ever mentioned that to me... why did she keep that a secret? And why was mum here? With you... I can't make any sense of all this."

Jacques looked up sharply from his glass and straight into my eyes. I don't think that he had expected me to be so direct. I'd touched a nerve or a wound that was still raw, sore, unhealed.

"What makes you think that, Marianne?"

We were stepping around each other with the things we weren't saying. Not quite on eggshells, but each knowing that what the other knew about my mother was dear to them. Our individual memories of her were fragile things.

"Well... when I was going through grandmas things, I found a photograph... of mum and a man... taken in somewhere called Saint Girons... in October 1943... here it is."

I placed the picture on the table. He stared at it, then tenderly picked it up and held it closer for inspection. He retrieved a pair of gold-framed spectacles from his pocket, cleaned them with a white cotton handkerchief and placed them on his nose. Ghosts of memories passed over his face. They rested in his eyes. A shadow of sadness descended on his shoulders as he sat back in the green and white padded garden chair. He looked up and across the patio towards a large terracotta planter with a substantial plant in bloom with delicate pink and cream flowers cascading from it.

"Do you see that plant in the container there? The variety is Valérie... I could not resist it when I saw it... c'est beau, is it not?" He smiled at the plant wistfully.

"It is beautiful... my mother must have made an impression on you... one that you have not forgotten."

"She did, I have never forgotten her Marianne..."

"Did you post this photograph to grandma? I think I must have been about seven years old when she received it."

"Yes, I did."

"Forgive me, Jacques, but why does the photo say the names Lucille and Claude when they aren't the names of the people in it. And is the date..."

Suddenly I couldn't form the words I needed to say into a sentence that would be coherent. The question I wanted to ask about her refused to rise in my throat, and yet it demanded to leave my head. It needed setting free into the world, and yet I was drowning under the tide of thoughts that I may have to face a new reality.

"Forgive me for interrupting, but what Marianne needs to know is... is Valérie alive?" Janet came to my rescue and hauled me from the spinning waters of my thoughts.

Jacques frowned first at Janet and then at me. "Why would you think that, Marianne?"

"Because... I don't know, something doesn't add up... I think someone made a mistake."

With a shaking hand, I retrieved the telegram from the ancient envelope in my handbag. I carefully opened it up and place it between us on the table next to the photograph.

"No, there is no mistake, my dear."

"But why does the telegram say she died in September 1943, when the picture is dated in October? It makes little sense at all... there must be a mistake."

I watched him closely. Jacques sighed as his fingers brushed over the photograph and the telegram. Did he think he could magic up mum? Like the genie from a lamp?

"The date of the picture is correct, I assure you. That is my handwriting, Marianne."

"But... but that means that mum was still alive when grandma had been told that she was dead?" I stared at him, dumbfounded. What did this mean? "So... why on earth would we have received a telegram telling us she had died in September? Jacques... I really don't understand."

"Ah, I cannot say for definite about the telegram your grandmother received. Your Government may have secretly condoned this course of action... but we lived in different times then... people had to make quick decisions in wartime, by the authorities on both sides of the Channel."

Jacques reached across the table and cradled my hand.

"I don't know the reasons they sent the telegram. Perhaps it could have been a genuine error, perhaps it was a deliberate attempt to cover up the truth... I really don't know... but either way, they sent a telegram to tell Winnie that Valérie had died. Marianne - she did not survive the war. I am sorry."

I let go of his hand. I walked to the edge of the patio, admiring the beautiful garden, needing to anchor my fluttering thoughts in something tangible, something grounded. My briefly raised hopes of the last few days now shattered and scattered about. My longed-for mother returned to history, laid to rest again in the past. And it was a relief. Returning to my seat, I refilled our glasses and took a sip.

"By the way... your mother loved lemonade too."

Looking at this gentle old man I felt as though, however unlikely, I was being given a window into some past events which I nor grandma had known. He seemed burdened by what he knew: as though he was facing the enormity of a task he was about to perform. I coaxed him gently from his faraway stare.

"So, what was my mum doing in France with you in October 1943, Jacques? I know the photograph is the clue... and I've seen the fact that things are not what they seem... am I correct?"

"Marianne, what I am about to tell you is true and is how I remember it after all these years... a lifetime ago now, yet I can vividly remember the first time I met her."

35

Marianne

Learning the truth

"Marianne I know that some of this seems too far-fetched to be true but please believe me, it is all true... Lucille, I'm sorry I often think of her as that, I mean Valérie, she was a saboteur and a mountain escort. She became a passeur, helping the French Resistance to escort others to freedom... she was in France but a short time. You should be proud of her... I was... she was... Une femme remarquable."

I stared at the old man in a look of disbelief. But there were still so many unanswered questions for me.

"She was a what? What did she do? What happened to her?"

"Aah, now that my dear, is an interesting question indeed... I believed she had left France after we crossed the Pyrenees together. I sent this photograph with a letter to her. Valérie had given me your address as we parted in Spain. We both knew that it was a dangerous thing to do and so I memorised it."

The deep sadness returned to his eyes and spilled across his face. His affection for my mother was clear. The realisation that mum had meant so much to Jacques touched me with a new sorrow. I could feel tears threatening to break free.

"I had hoped to come to England after the war, to see her. But your grandmother wrote back to me, thanking me for the photograph and informing me that Valérie had died in September at an RAF base. I was just as confused as you have been since seeing the discrepancy."

The pain of his discovery of my mother's death was in his eyes and etched into every wrinkle in his face. He too had lived with a memory of my missing mother.

"I knew something was amiss, the date was incorrect... and I knew I could not say that to your grandmother without having a correct explanation for her. And for you."

We were silent for a few moments more. I stood up and went to the edge of the patio area. The horrors and darkness of the acts of war that my mother must have seen, but I did not know about, were in such sharp contrast with this delightful garden, full of sunshine and colour. It all seemed a lifetime ago, and yet the memory of the day the telegram arrived was as clear as if it were yesterday.

"So, tell me what happened to her Jacques. I need to know... please. I can only guess at how painful and upsetting this must be for you."

"I have carried this for many years... I have saved it close to me, hoping that one day I could tell you the truth, but I didn't know where to begin or how to do it. Then the years went by, and the memories faded a little... And so perhaps I have been a coward in some ways... you deserved to know before today. I'm sorry, Marianne."

"No, you have not been a coward, it is obviously painful for you to tell me these things. Please, do not apologise... go on," I encouraged him again. Using the word coward struck me as odd - when would it ever have been the right time to tell a child of sad and painful events?

Protecting me from this wasn't a cowardly act. It had been a brave decision on his part.

"After receiving your grandmother's letter, I travelled to St. Girons and tried to find anyone who was still there, anyone from our network. It was only about a year after the war ceased. I wanted to find out if anyone knew what had happened to her... but I could find no one. People seemed reluctant to talk to an outsider, a stranger who asked questions about the Resistance... The café owner said that he had heard that some in our group at the safe house that your mother had used... they disappeared, arrested. The Nazis tortured then shot them. Presumably so that they could not help the Allies as they approached. The contacts and people in our network seemed to have gone. I was just about to give up on finding out any information."

I looked at him and could see that the dark clouds of those days had passed over his memory again. I knew I had to wait patiently until they receded from his thoughts and revealed their secrets from the shadows.

Jacques cleared his throat and blinked away tears.

"It was quite by chance that I saw Monsieur Henri the butcher crossing the square. I had already paid a visit to his shop, but a new family owned it after the war and they thought he had gone to live near Toulouse. I hurried after him, I was a lot younger in those days, my dear." He smiled broadly at this memory.

I could picture him over fifty years ago as the younger, agile man with my mother in the photograph. Then I realised I had heard that name before, at the museum in London.

"Was that Albert Henri?"

Jacques jerked up his head and the look of surprise alarmed me. I had truly touched the raw nerve of a painful memory.

"Albert was the son of the butcher... he was executed in the village square after we destroyed the bridge. But... how do you know that name Marianne?"

"Janet and I went to an exhibition at the War Museum to find out some information about the WAAF and what mum might have done in it. We saw some footage of her and a man outside a church, they were laughing... and when I asked the curator where the film had come from they showed us the tin it was kept in. It had the name Albert Henri written on it. And... and... the man in the film was you, wasn't it? Did you catch up with Monsieur Henri?"

"Of course I did! I was a fit young man then, and we waste youth on the young... Monsieur Henri was astounded to see me, as I was him. He knew they had moved me into another circuit of Resistants after I had returned from the mountain crossing with Lucille and Manuel and Elena. He had presumed that I had returned to my home in Perpignan after the war. Which I had."

"So what did Monsieur Henri tell you? Did he know what had happened to her?"

"It was purely by chance he was there that day. He had a solicitor's appointment about the adoption of the orphaned Jewish boy he had taken under his wing. But no, he didn't know what had happened to her. But he told me that Valérie did not return to Saint Girons as far as he was aware. He believed that there were two more successful but cruel crossings of the Pyrenees after ours. He said that he presumed Valérie must have either been part of them somewhere along the route, that she had escaped to return to England… or that they had arrested her."

My heart was pounding at the thought of this as a reality of her death. The possibility that they had arrested her, or tortured – or both – and killed her seemed unreal. An involuntary gasp escaped from my mouth. The anguish that I felt for her set free into the world.

"Oh Marianne, please do not fret, I found out the truth within a few days."

Was I ready to hear the truth? The unclear path of it had led me to London and now to France, it had given me sleepless nights and then the false hope of mum's survival. I finished the remains of my lemonade and poured us each a fresh glass. Janet had sat silently through the unfolding story. I saw she was taking notes and making small sketches in her ever-present notebook.

"Thank you, Marianne. Shall I continue? We can take a break if you wish, I understand that this is a lot of extra information for you to take in." He raised his glass and took a sip.

I nodded. I was about to step through the gates into a new world of truth.

"I remember we shared coffee and a poor quality cognac, it did not impress Monsieur Henri… I think he had received some, how do you say it in English? Perks? By trading with the Nazis in the war. But we all had to do what we had to do to stay alive."

Jacques' voice trailed off as he recalled distant memories and events.

"And then what did you do?"

"Then I planned. I knew it was probably a long shot, as you say in English, but I wondered whether I could find the Spaniards, Elena and Manuel, the mountain guides who had helped us escape from France. They'd taken us over the Pyrenees. And so I travelled to Esterri d'Aneu, over the border in Spain. It's the nearest town to Alos d'Isil, about 12km away if my memory serves me correctly."

"So Jacques, forgive me if I'm not understanding you correctly... so you're telling me that my mum escaped from France with you over the mountains?"

"Yes, I am. It was after we had destroyed the bridge in Saint Girons, the German authorities in the region ordered reprisals. It was a common eye for an eye tactic. They rounded up some townspeople and in doing so they captured some of our Resistance comrades. They executed them... so it was not safe for your Maman and I to remain there. We had to leave immediately, and the escape line over the mountains was the obvious, indeed the only option."

This revelation shocked me. My mum had been a million miles from the comparative safety of an underground listening facility on the south coast where I believed she had been.

"And did you find the Spanish guides?"

"It took me a couple of days to reach my destination, transport and travel and roads did not magically reappear after the official end of the war in 1945... many of us, all across Europe lived within the meagre food rations and harsh conditions we had endured during the war for many years afterwards... but I finally reached Esterri d'Aneu late one evening."

"But how did you know where to look for two Spanish people when you did not know their actual names or addresses?"

Genuinely intrigued and in awe of this man before me, I understood his longing and need to find out what had happened to the woman he knew as Lucille, my mum. I now believed he had carried a candle for her, for what? Their wartime encounter? The years afterwards? His lifetime? The thought touched my heart with tenderness and affection. This stranger now felt like a friend. His willingness to share his knowledge and memories of mum with me was obviously difficult for him.

"Ah, Marianne - we were the people of the Resistance, the marquisards, we had learnt to be unseen. We were resourceful at making something out of nothing, of creating and inventing ways to make plans: the masters of illusion, we could make things and people disappear into thin air. And by the same token we could create personalities, real-life characters that lived in a community as if they had lived there all their lives. We knew how to find out things, people, information – and our Spanish counterparts did the same. I just hoped that I had not lost my skills when I arrived there."

I laughed at the thought of this. The man in front of me was an illusionist: I would not have been in the least bit surprised if he had pulled a rabbit out of his pocket.

"So the next day I went to the local café and town hall offices and asked questions about the local families. I remembered that Manuel and Elena had said they were siblings and that their father was a farmer. And again, by chance the café owner recalled that the local seamstress might help me, she had relations who had been farmers near Alos d'Isil. He gave me directions to her shop. It was close by, I think... my memory does not serve me so well sometimes."

By now I felt I was getting closer to the truth and the people who had last seen mum alive. I felt an anxiety rising in the tightness in my chest. A fear of an intangible unknown.

"When I reached her little sewing shop, she was just pulling the tattered blind down on the door and about to close up for siesta... but I was insistent that she opened the door again. When she did, I recognised something about her, a similarity to the young Elena. The seamstress was hesitant to reveal any details... which I suppose was understandable as there were still reprisals happening, there was bitterness about collaborators and even people who denied that the Resistance movement had existed... eventually when I mentioned Manuel's little brown terrier dog she smiled and shook my hand. She told me that only the special helpers knew about the little dog... and that she was their Aunt and that their Uncle had also been a mountain guide."

I let out an enormous sigh, realising that I had been holding my breath. I stretched out my shoulders that had become hunched and tense as Jacques told his story, my mother's story. Theirs were intertwined tales.

"Did she tell you where to find Elena and Manuel? It must have been nerve-wracking for you – to be so near, yet so far from possibly finding them."

"Yes, she told me to cross the street and catch the bus. I was to tell the driver to stop at the Ortiz farmland. Then she handed me a neatly wrapped parcel and asked me to give it to Elena... it was a dress I think... it was such a relief to have found someone who knew the passeurs, the brave guides of the mountains, who might tell me what had happened to Valérie."

I could almost picture Jacques standing at the bus stop with a brown paper parcel, getting closer to the truth – as I was too.

"When the bus reached the place that I was looking for, the driver told me to follow the dirt track road to the farmhouse in the distance. When I reached it, there was no one around in the farmyard but as I say it was siesta time. So I sat down against a stone wall in the shade. After a while I heard someone open a door and as I stood up a little dog barked loudly at me, I startled it I think. I was in the right place – Manuel stood outside lighting a cigarette and the dog was jumping up with excitement at my side."

"Did he recognise you? Manuel I mean."

"Yes, he looked at me and I remember he called me Claude... and rushed to me. We hugged. He looked older somehow, a sadness in his eyes, although it was only three years since I had seen him... he made me some strong coffee and told me that his sister Elena lived there with him. She was out in the fields. Eventually he asked me why I had come... and I asked him what had happened to Valérie."

"Oh Jacques, it must have been a tough question for you to ask... what did he say? Did he know?"

"Marianne it was crucial that I found out – I knew your grandmother was living under a lie, although she didn't know it... and your mother's bravery deserved the truth, someone had to know it, so that it was out there and existed in the world."

Jacques took a deep breath as though he was preparing for something, to say something important. He reached across and held my hand.

"Manuel told me that after our crossing, Valérie had stayed with them in a safe house for a week. It was back up the valley. I had last seen Valérie when we had parted at the safe house in Alos d'Isil. I had to leave to help another escape line, called the Pat Line, after Pat O'Leary... that route ran over the eastern section of the Pyrenees from Perpignan... I eventually returned home via that route... I left her alone in that farmhouse."

The painful memories revealed themselves in his eyes as his body shrank a little with some untold misery that I would never know – or understand. We were silent for a few moments, and then I gently stroked his hand to bring him back to his task of telling.

"Aah, yes... where was I? I'm sorry Marianne, the memories when they come back – sometimes they're clear, all in colour. Many people think of the war being fought in black and white because few photos were in colour then... anyway, I digress. So where was I?... Manuel told me that your mother had rested for a week. She'd told him she did not want to return to England just yet, and that her intention was to help them escort another party over the high pass to freedom in Spain, by the same route. The local organisers, Manuel said, were happy to have her as she had proved capable of making the dangerous trip."

His words disturbed me. Especially the use of 'her intention' – implying that this was an unfinished act, a plan that wasn't completed.

"And so Valérie headed back up the mountains through the high pass at Col de la Pale de la Clauer and over the border, back into France. When Elena, Manuel and Valérie reached the shelter hut at Refuge des Estagnous, he said that they agreed it was more sensible for her to wait there for two days for them to return with their next packets. This is what we called the evaders. It would conserve the negligible amount of food they had and the energy of one of them. They told her they would ask their contact to get a message to London to let them know she was assisting the escape lines... and so they left her behind there in the mountain hut."

"Oh!" The unintended sound I made was a cross between a gasp and whisper. The thought of her being high in the mountains, all alone, saddened me. Or was it just a reflection of my loneliness and sadness when I was waiting for her to come back?

"Marianne my dear... what I will tell you next – well, there isn't a way to tell you that won't shock you I'm afraid." His voice trailed off, and he looked out across the garden. It was his turn to take my hand this time.

"Go on, it's ok... just tell me the truth Jacques."

"When they returned to the refuge hut with the next group of escapees, they could not find her at first. Manuel said that the fresh footprints in the snow told them that others had been there... at first they thought the Germans had arrested her – or the Spanish... they did not know. But despite the danger, the group had to rest there for a while, exhausted... then it was Elena who found her when she went round the back of the little outhouse. They had shot her, a single bullet in the back of her head."

"Oh, Jacques!... No! Not after her bravery and sacrifice, no."

The tears rolled down both of our cheeks for the sadness and utter waste of my mum's young life.

I could not speak, and Janet came to my side and held me. Several minutes passed as we both recovered our composure. Was it better to die in a bomb released by a nameless aircraft operator or by a single bullet from a rifle held by a man you could not look in the eyes? I could not comprehend the state of mind or motivation of either perpetrators. But as Jacques had said, 'times were different in war.' I had the benefit of growing up in peaceful times. The paradox was that both the killer and the deceased both believed that they were fighting for the right cause and opposing versions of peace.

Jacques cleared his throat, "There was one very odd thing though - Manuel noticed she held a button in her hand, now let me find it... ah, here it is. What made it odd was that it had not fallen off her coat."

He carefully removed a small, once blue button from the breast pocket of his shirt and placed it on top of the photograph.

I recognised it instantly. It transfixed me, I could not, dared not move.

"Marianne? Do you recognise the button?"

"Yes," I whispered. "It was the eye on my rag doll when I was a child... it came off one day, I think it was the day she took me to the park and I fell over and cut my knee, I'm not sure... and grandma was sure that it was in her button tin when she went to stitch it back on... but she never found it there... why would Maman have taken my rag doll's missing eye to France with her?"

"I can only think that she had it hidden in the lining of her clothes, as a reminder of you, Marianne. The British agents couldn't bring any belongings with them, no photographs, nothing... if captured and something identified them as not being French... it would mean death for them. She must have hidden it somewhere when she left England."

I picked it up and fingered the faded wooden disc between my finger and thumb, marvelling again at her bravery. I had such a connection with her in that moment that a smile took over my face.

"Thank you, Jacques... thank you for saving these memories for me."

"Please take the button it belongs to you."

My thank you did not seem big enough. It felt inadequate compared to what these people had endured during that cruel time.

Jacques tried to stand up from his seat but struggled to pull himself out of it. I went around the table and helped him up.

"Damned old age! Come, let us walk around the garden and not be so sad. Let us be happy for what we achieved in France."

As we quietly strolled, in my mind I could only see the woman in the photograph – alive, young, vibrant - and not a dead body alone in the snow on a French mountain. And the same for Jacques – I pictured an active, passionate, fit young man. They must have made a handsome couple – if ever they were. I did not need to know. This man was special to me now.

We had arrived at the patio again, and Jacques obviously needed to sit down. He said that his legs and each passing year reminded him daily that the new day was a gift. A guaranteed tomorrow wasn't possible either.

We sipped the rest of the now warm lemonade.

"But there's still one thing I don't quite understand, Jacques... why did the telegram arrive to say she had died in September 1943 when she was clearly still alive in the photograph of you both in October? How could the War Office or whoever sent the telegrams out – how could they send such dreadful news to a family when it wasn't true? It seems cruel."

"Ah Marianne, I asked myself the same question for many years and I couldn't find an answer. The world differed from now, and they decided quickly in wartime... but eventually I came to believe that the British authorities thought she was dead. Think about it - they knew they had dropped her into France as a radio operator and saboteur. They knew she had made her way to St. Girons. She had sent messages from there. And then the messages had stopped abruptly when we had to leave. We did not know whether some arrested Resistants shot in the square had revealed our Resistance network in the area. We did not know whether they had betrayed us."

"But something about it still makes little sense Jacques – surely London would have waited to hear from her or from another network, a radio message or something."

"It turns out that the truth was simple Marianne – the bombing of the air base, that was the cover for her stationing, by a Luftwaffe raid on the 28th of September killed several people. But your mother was not there. She was at RAF Tempsford in Bedfordshire, waiting to be despatched as an SOE agent. She took off from there on the evening of the 29th of September. I was the leader of the reception party in the French field she parachuted into that night."

"But that does not mean that,"

"What it means, my dear Marianne, is that the RAF would have concentrated on getting its operations going again as quickly as possible after the bombing of the airbase. That was the utmost priority.

Casualties were probably a secondary thought... the key thing was to get aircraft back in the air. The sooner they did that, the more people they protected from air raids. The department that handled the SOE agents would have become more concerned about her silence... they must have presumed the worst... the telegram about the bombing of the base was convenient. Remember, no one knew about these agents, they were secret people, hidden from sight, they had disappeared from their everyday lives into a secret organisation. No one knew, nor would believe, that women were being trained to kill and fight the Axis invaders in France."

"Ah, I see – so the timing of things was all very convenient for the SOE commanders and protected their hidden status as a department. You almost couldn't make it up, could you?" I smiled at Jacques.

"You're right, you probably couldn't... I thought that by sending the photograph to your grandmother that she might see the differences in the dates and perhaps ask some questions of the authorities. But I suppose she had lost her daughter, and you were her life. She had a duty to Valérie to look after you."

"If she had noticed the dates, she never ever mentioned a word to me. And none of it would have brought my mum back, anyway."

"That is true, Marianne. Valérie's story and that of the other women agents and what they risked their lives for is also true. It is a truth that the free world should not forget," he replied.

AND SO...

The truth was revealed to me at last. The enormity of mother's courage and sacrifice astounded me. My thanks to Jacques for holding this precious memory and reality of her over the years seemed somehow to be an unequal and inadequate exchange. A simple 'Thank you' was not enough to express my gratitude to him.

And so, sometimes when the truth about someone you know turns out to be bigger than you could have imagined, you're humbled. The infinite capacity of the human heart and spirit when it looks fear and ultimately death in its face staggered and amazed me.

As Janet and I left Jacques later that evening, my head was spinning at the revelations. I had a completely new respect and profound love for the woman I had never known yet was part of me. The thought of mum as one of many women who served within the SOE and made the ultimate sacrifice filled me with pride. And a determination to record the awful events and their achievements. Jacques agreed to write his memories of the awful events he and mum had witnessed as Claude and Lucille. And we planned to publish them.

At last, the missing mother of my childhood was real, no longer just a collection of black and white photographs and frozen snapshots in time held in a compartment in my mind. I had replaced the loneliness and longing for a long absent person. I had filled it with the essence of a living woman who had warmth and was in colour. A woman with a personality and fears and doubts, just like me.

And this new knowledge of her was a gift of great peace and healing.

Perhaps the next adventure on the path of truth is to find out who my father was...

ABOUT THE AUTHOR AND THIS BOOK

The childhood loss of a parent leaves a scar of deep grief and sadness. These are painful feelings to express at any age. This is something I experienced at an early age: my mother died aged 25. I was nearly five years old. I was far too young to understand or deal with the thoughts and emotions then. And so over the years I had developed coping mechanisms for them and had thought that as time passed, I'd safely distanced myself from them. But I was wrong.

In 2019/20 I worked with a business and book doula for my fledgling freelance copy-editing and proofreading business. This wonderful woman together with some close friends showed me it was actually my real and exposed self with all my feelings that needed to be born into its truest expression in the world first. And by doing so, healing the grief and loss would follow. And then business would come to be because of this. Part of this process would be to write the book I've always wanted to write. And so, here it is – my gift to myself. And to you.

Losing a parent at an incredibly young age teaches you either to believe in fairy tales and happily ever after, or it gives you a strong sense of self preservation and survival in life. I know that I never really believed in fairy tales.

As I had a significant half century birthday, I realised that I actually knew little about this woman who had given birth to me. It also dawned on me I had survived in this life for twice as many years as her too brief life. From snippets of information I gleaned over the years from family members, I pictured a woman with a strong character, with a caring and friendly personality, but little more than that. My family comprised mainly male relatives. They always seemed reluctant to talk to me about her in some ways, they were carrying their own pain. Now I look back I think I must have been a reminder of her as I look like her. And so, over the years she faded, no one spoke of her: where it felt like she had not existed, she had disappeared. She was 'missing.'

And then one day I thought, "Hang on, what if this woman had been truly remarkable and no one ever knew? Or no one has told me? What if she had been a pioneering scientist? An archaeologist who had discovered a great treasure? Or a spy or a secret agent?" Perhaps I had an undiscovered need to believe in fairy tales after all...

And so the idea of telling my story of loss had now found a setting, a background in which I could reveal it. I had originally thought of her as the first female James Bond type of character, but I don't really go in for all of this product placement and fast car stuff. So Jane Bond wasn't born.

Around this time I had read a fascinating book - Cruel Crossing by Edward Stourton. It is a book that has stayed with me, hopefully for the right reasons. It bought to light for me the increasingly forgotten bravery of those ordinary people in Europe who resisted the Nazi occupation. Their active resistance to the regime was literally as life threatening as it was heroic as they escorted Jewish families of all nationalities, British soldiers and RAF pilots and crew, American airmen across the Pyrenees to relative safety.

Edward's book refers to Nancy Wake aka the White Mouse who had led groups of escapees across the mountains. She also escaped the Gestapo on at least two occasions. This woman's bravery and courage fascinated me, and I researched into her life. This led me to the history of the Special Operations Executive known as the SOE, and in particular the women that played their amazing – if unbelievably true – part in defeating the rise of the Nazis.

The story of the female SOE operatives is as fascinating as it is harrowing. Of the 52 women engaged in this type of war work, 12 never returned. "Thirty-nine women from French Section went to war, and fourteen died in action. While the casualty rate seems high, war is always deadly for forward units in particular."

These were ordinary women – wives, sisters, daughters, mothers. Women like me (and perhaps you). The sad and disturbing element of this is the fact that the real, detailed story of these women did not receive the public or authorities' recognition of their commitment and bravery until many years later. During the 1950s there was still a reluctance, in some official quarters, to give proper recognition to them with military honours. The conventions of war classed them as civilians. They served a cause they believed to be just with no less passion, bravery and commitment than male fighting soldiers, sailors and airmen. With hindsight it is easy to say that some should have received the rightly deserved honours sooner, but times differed from our informed expectations now. This is not to dismiss the lack of lasting recognition by the authorities, more a product of the age that some of them survived and lived through. At the time of their recruitment to the SOE, women could not take up armed combat in war despite the recognised valuable support roles they had provided during World War One. Unbelievably combat roles remained closed to female soldiers until 2016.

And so I hope that by setting a very personal story of grief and loss against factual events I might prompt you to discover for yourself, perhaps for the first time, the truly remarkable yet real story of the SOE women.

However, please understand that my story is purely fictional. It was created in my imagination, then transferred to paper from historical research and extensive reading. Any errors, omissions and stretching of the facts, characters and situations to fit this story are entirely of my doing. The story is my own life experiences and my own feelings within this setting.

There is no intention in any meaning, implication, or intention to undermine, demean, or lessen the huge and lasting contribution of the true heroines who served their country to bring the restoration of peace and freedom for us all.

And in securing peace for us, they truly have enabled their daughters and granddaughters to raise their voices and tell their own stories. Thank you.

ACKNOWLEDGEMENTS

In no particular order, my heartfelt gratitude goes to:

Rev Dr Sidney Bindemann – who was both a gentleman and a gentle man who, through his tenacity and strength, showed me you are never too old to follow your dream, especially if it is to publish your own story.

Debbie Instone – we met in 1969 as five- and four-year-olds, my oldest and truest friend who has never changed. Thank you for your lasting friendship reflected in your reading of my first untidy and disorganised draft. And your unending encouragement and support of this project.

Special thanks and love go to the ladies of the Dragon Writers Group – our shared silences across the globe have been as loud as the roars of the dragon. Go tell your stories, ladies.

Saveria Freedom and the support received within the Wise Women Writing Womb.

My ever grateful thanks go to John Seymour of Write Now for his critique of my draft novella of 35,000 words. Your encouragement to expand it into a novel happened! Also to the members of John's Newcastle Writers Group – you're all fantastically inspirational writers.

Mark Richards – the person who set me off on this whole copy-editing and writing malarkey! Your inspiration and honest encouragement cannot be underestimated and was always tempered with Ernest Hemingway's words "Once writing has become your major vice and greatest pleasure, only death can stop it."

Tracey Digby – for introducing me to the delightfully vintage Gladys Tea Rooms in Hartlepool that I used in the book. It was just the setting that I imagined Valérie and Eleanor in, having their last cup of tea in 1943.

To the talented 'technical crew' of Linnhe Harrison at 2 Bears Creative who, together with Dennis Sisterson, dealt with making the cover design and the internal maps. My heartfelt thanks to you both for turning the pictures in my head into the reality of a book cover.

And to my fellow yogi Kate Pattinson, whose input on the final back cover wording was perfect and proves that a second pair of eyes is priceless. Thank you.

With gratitude to both Zoe James at Blooming Bamboo Yoga, Seaham and Elaine Smith at Hot Pod Yoga, Sunderland, for your endless encouragement and listening ears when I've wittered on for far too long about this project. Your gifts of breathing and space have carried me through when things have been tough going. Thank you.

And to all my amazing friends, family, sea dippers, online class yogis and walking buddies. Thank you does not seem enough for your unstinting support and ongoing interest in my project that has turned into a published book. My original intention was for one printed copy for myself.

And last but certainly not the least of all these was Valérie Ann Webb nee Siviter b. 1944, who died 21st January 1969. You gave me life – and an imagination, thank you x.

FURTHER READING AND RESEARCH RESOURCES USED

Childhood bereavement

The wonderful work of the UK childhood loss charity can be seen at

https://www.childbereavementuk.org/

Shockingly their most recent statistics show that a parent of children under 18 dies every 22 minutes in the UK; that's around 23,600 a year. This equates to around 111 children being bereaved of a parent every day.

1 in 29 of 5-16-year-olds has been bereaved of a parent or sibling - that's a child in every average class.

Special Operations Executive

An Overview of Special Operations Executive

In 1942, the Allies were losing, Germany seemed unstoppable, and every able man in England was fighting. Churchill believed Britain was locked in an existential battle and created a secret agency, the Special Operations Executive (SOE), whose operatives were trained in everything from demolition to sharp-shooting. Their job, he declared, was "to set Europe ablaze!" But with most men on the front lines, the SOE did something unprecedented: it recruited women. Thirty-nine women answered the call, leaving their lives and families to become saboteurs in France. Half were caught, and a third did not make it home alive.

Books used in my SOE research:

Special Operations Executive... How to be an Agent in Occupied Europe, from The National Archives, William Collins, 2014.

D Day Girls, The Spies Who Armed the Resistance, Sabotaged the Nazis, and Helped Win World War II by Sarah Rose, Crown New York, 2019.

Nancy Wake: Soe's Greatest Heroine by Russell Braddon, The History Press, 2009.

Heroines of the SOE: Britain's Secret Women in France F Section by Squadron Leader Beryl E Escott, The History Press, 2012.

Violet Szabo: The life that I have by Susan Ottaway, Thistle Publishing, 2014.

A Life in Secrets: The Story of Vera Atkins and the Lost Agents of SOE by Sarah Helm, Abacus, 2006.

Websites used:

https://www.culture24.org.uk/history-and-heritage/military-history/world-war-two/tra14553

http://www.bbc.co.uk/history/worldwars/wwtwo/soe_01.shtml

https://spartacus-educational.com/2WWsoe.htm

https://www.nationalgeographic.com/news/2014/11/141119-special-operations-executive-soe-world-war-women-ngbooktalk/

https://www.historic-uk.com/HistoryUK/HistoryofBritain/The-Female-Spies-Of-SOE/

https://en.wikipedia.org/wiki/List_of_female_SOE_agents

https://www.thegazette.co.uk/awards-and-accreditation/content/100273

https://www.encyclopedia.com/history/encyclopedias-almanacs-transcripts-and-maps/atkins-vera

http://www.thenewforestguide.co.uk/history/new-forest-at-war/new-forest-ww2

https://en.wikipedia.org/wiki/Special_Operations_Executive#Leadership

http://www.bbc.co.uk/history/worldwars/wwtwo/soe_training_01.shtml

For general WWII living conditions:
https://www.1900s.org.uk/war.htm

The Freedom Trail

Books used in my research:
Cruel Crossing: Escaping Hitler Across the Pyrenees by Edward Stourton, Black Swan, 2014.

The Freedom Trail: Following one of the hardest wartime routes across the central Pyrenees into Northern Spain by Scott Goodall, Inchmere Design, 2005.

With special thanks to Scott's son, Alistair, for supplying this book and some background on his father's excellent guide.

Escaping Hitler: Heroic True Stories of Great Escapes in Nazi Europe by Monty Halls, Pan Books, 2018.

The Resistance: the French Fight Against the Nazis by Matthew Cobb, Pocket Books, 2009.

Websites used in my research:
An excellent website can be found at https://www.chemindelaliberte.fr/

This is the official site of The Freedom Route (I suggest you translate it in to English). It details the route between Saint Girons in France and Esterri d'Àneu in Spain with lots of background information. Each year the Chemin Association organises a commemorative hike in the footsteps of those who refused Nazi oppression during the last world conflict.

And the equally informative https://ww2escapelines.co.uk/ offers a wealth of thought-provoking information, which is being preserved for future generations.

May we nor our children or grandchildren ever see these trails and escape routes being used again for their original purpose.